I0747983

GRACE DESIGNS MYSTERIES

Seams Like Murder

TILLY WALLACE

Copyright © 2023 by Tilly Wallace

All rights reserved.

No part of this book may be reproduced in any form or by any electronic or mechanical means, including information storage and retrieval systems, without written permission from the author, except for the use of brief quotations in a book review.

v18072023

Print ISBN: 978-1-7385845-2-9

Cover design by Melody Simmons

Editing Kat's Literary Services

To be the first to hear about Tilly's new releases and exclusive offers, sign up at:

https://www.tillywallace.com/newsletter

This book uses British English, a dollop of Downunder English, and a scattering of Kiwi idioms

Chapter One

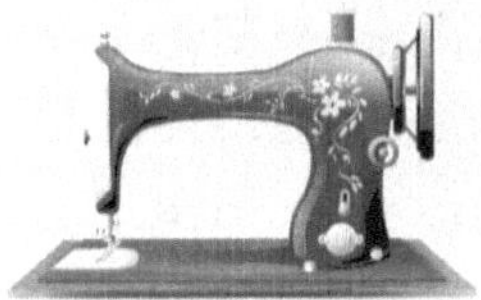

Thursday, 15 January 1920
Wellington, NEW ZEALAND

MY DAD ALWAYS TOLD ME TO DO SOMETHING YOU love, and you'll never regret a day of work. He was right. At least about that. From a young age, I had delighted in sewing. The ability to take a length of cloth and create anything I wanted possessed a kind of magic. Then events that should have ruined my life, instead opened up the opportunity to start my own tiny fashion house—Grace Designs.

My humble business occupied the bottom corner of a building on Plimmer Steps, a cobbled lane that ran from Lambton Quay to Boulcott Street. Every day, numerous pedestrians used the shortcut between the buildings and up the steep stairs. My workshop occupied a space before the wide window. The large cutting table, made by my dad, occupied the centre of the room. Against one wall sat my Singer sewing machine. A dress form either side. A private room for fittings was secluded on the other side of the room. A glass top bench stretched out near the rear of the shop.

Today I worked alone. My assistant Etáin Doyle, or Etty, had the most terrible head cold, and I didn't want her nose dripping onto delicate silk. With hand stitching on my lap, I sat in a chair placed in the light coming through the window. A wooden workbox open on the small table beside me. Sometimes, a curious passer-by would pause and stare at the item I was sewing.

I felled a seam on the skirt of a walking ensemble—tedious work that some seamstresses didn't bother with. After pressing the seam open, I turned the edge on either side under and pinned it down. Then another pass with the iron kept hot on the small potbelly in the corner of the room. Now, a tiny row of stitches marched along the fabric and finished the edge. My mentor, Mrs Cooper, always told me it was the invisible details that distinguished a fine haute couture gown from mass-produced fashion. Work that required patience and care, like felling a seam.

On my left hand, the one holding the fabric, I had drawn two black lines on my thumbnail. Those lines acted as a tiny measure and ensured every stitch was the exact same size. The repetitive nature of the work induced a kind of trance state. My inhales and exhales matched the needle being passed through the linen. I finished off the row and snipped the thread as the brass bell above the door tinkled.

A blast of warm January summer air burst into my shop, along with a customer who sent dread flowing through my limbs. A willowy form clad in a fashionable day dress of yellow stripe with a wide sailor collar and a smart matching straw hat marched in. She was exactly the sort of customer I longed to see walk through my door. Except for this particular person.

I had nothing personal against Agatha Marshall. She was overall a lovely person, quick to smile or offer a kind word. My issue with Agatha resided entirely with her memory. She would forget an appointment and leave me waiting for hours. Or she would forget how much she adored the blue silk and insist on green chiffon. Or she would forget to pay her rather large and outstanding bill which meant I had to pare back a recent fabric order from England.

"My darling Grace! It's been absolutely ages!" Agatha swanned into my little shop and reached out to touch the tweed draped on the dress form for an outfit perfect for cold winter days.

It had been ages because she still hadn't paid her bill, and I had fobbed off all her attempts to book a fitting.

"Hello, Miss Marshall. You are looking lovely today." I placed the skirt pieces into my work basket and rose.

The bright yellow of Agatha's dress combined with her large smile reminded me of a sunflower.

"I need your help, Grace, and you are the only one who can help me out of this pickle." She dropped to the comfortable leather armchair, reserved for customers as they were shown sketches or fabric. She clutched her purse on her lap and her fingers fidgeted with the golden catch.

"Oh?" Her dress didn't appear to need any repair and I recalled seeing it as part of the new summer collection at Kirkcaldie and Stains—the premier department store in Wellington.

"I am dying for the starring role in Liam's new show at the Cricket. Rumour has it that a hotshot Hollywood producer is in New Zealand for a holiday, and he will attend opening night!"

She practically squealed when she mentioned Hollywood. A place far away and not subject to chilly winters. Or so I had read in a magazine. Silent films were making stars from ordinary folk, and Agatha dreamed of appearing on the big screen one day. I'd never heard of any star coming from little old New Zealand, though. Not that we didn't have our share of talented folk, but it was a terribly long boat journey to America if you wanted to be discovered. Probably why she was so excited if a movie producer had slid down to our part of the globe.

"There is a grand party at Antrim House tonight and simply everybody who is anybody is going. I know if I can charm Liam, he will give the lead to me, and not that fumble-footed blonde. Imagine—Hollywood!" She managed to both exclaim and sigh over the last word.

My heart fell. Agatha not only wanted a new frock, but she expected it at incredibly short notice. "I'm sorry, Miss Marshall. I couldn't possibly make a gown by tonight." Not even if I wanted to, and you were going to pay me—in advance.

"But Grace, I need to look ravishing. I will simply die if I don't get this part and it goes to that cow, Mintie." At this point, she leaned back in the chair and pressed her hand to her forehead in a melodramatic fashion. She really was suited to life as a starlet, from her stunning looks to her extravagant gestures. Everything about her life was do or die.

However, my family would die if I didn't put food on the table. Which was exactly why I ran my own small fashion house, even though others would laugh at calling it such. Six years ago, as war broke out across Europe, I left my regular employment and took the risk of opening *Grace Designs*. I barely made enough during those years and supplemented my income by sewing uniforms, but now with war and the influenza pandemic behind us, things were looking up. There was a chance to expand and hire another seamstress.

"Have you been to see what Kirkcaldie and Stains have in stock? They released some lovely cocktail dresses over Christmas, up on the first floor." Once, I used to be a shop girl there. Then I rose to fittings and repairs before my departure. Thanks to Mrs Cooper who was not only a wealthy customer of the department store, she also owned the building where I rented my workroom.

"Oh, don't be so horrid, Grace! You know your dresses are the most sought-after these days. As I must be." Agatha closed her eyes and tilted her head back farther.

Agatha wasn't like the showgirls who danced and sang to entertain the late-night set. She came from a well-off family and could have married and lived a comfortable life that revolved around lunches and dress fittings. Instead, she pursued her dream of being a Hollywood star. But that required relocating from New Zealand to the bright lights and glamour of the United States of America. A journey her family refused to sanction or fund.

The showgirl was convinced that if she attracted the right attention in Wellington, she would be swept away to the life of a movie star in California. To rub shoulders with Rudolph Valentino and Gloria Swanson. Everyone had a dream, Agatha's simply involved more logistical problems.

"I am ever so sorry, Miss Marshall, but I simply couldn't complete an expensive commission like that in such a short amount of time," I emphasised the word *expensive*, hoping her horrendous memory would recall the outstanding account. Perhaps then her hands would dive into her designer clutch and pull out a wad of cash.

Agatha dropped her hand, but not to search the handbag for my outstanding money. Instead, she placed the bag on the seat and stood. She paced my workroom with a restless energy like a caged tiger at the

Wellington zoo. "You must have something tucked away, Grace? A little project for no particular client that could be made to fit with one of those new handkerchief hemlines and a chiffon train." She lifted a bolt of rust red chiffon and peered underneath as though suspecting it might unfold into a complete gown.

I did indeed have projects I worked on at night, or in my free time. On one, the metallic embroidery alone was taking me weeks. When completed, it would resemble the cheeky fantail where his distinctive tail was transformed into a curved train of burnished bronze, grey, and cream. Part of me longed for an occasion to wear it myself, but it would most likely find an owner among Wellington's inner circle of high society.

"No," I lied. "I don't have anything at all. Since you are here, there is the matter of your overdue account." Protecting the fantail gown emboldened me. She would never pay unless prodded along.

"You would trouble me about money at a time like this?" her voice rose to a sharp tone.

Pedestrians in the lane stopped. Agatha's waving arms and volume drew their attention.

I darted a glance at the growing audience. A dancer might be used to men staring at her performance, I was not. Nor did I want to air dirty laundry in the middle of town. The large window which had so appealed to me for allowing as much light into my rooms as possible, now became a stage and we were actors upon it.

"There is no need to shout, Miss Marshall. I don't think there is ever a good time to discuss finances, but the bill has been due for some time now. I cannot buy the fabrics I require for other customers until it is settled." My son, Theo, wanted nothing more than a bright red bicycle for his fifth birthday in April. I wanted to purchase a new one for him, but until Agatha paid her bill, we might have to settle for an old bicycle dad would restore and paint. One day, I vowed, my son would have new things and not hand-me-downs.

Agatha spun on me, her eyes wide. The bright light in them grew cold. "I happen to know that you are a liar, *Mrs Devine*. And you will find me a dress by tonight. Unless you want me to tell all of them your little lie?"

She flung out her arm and gestured to the crowd watching the show playing out in my window. They stared openly, perhaps trying to determine if they observed a comedy or a tragedy.

A chill worse than the Wellington southerly in the middle of winter froze my bones. I swallowed, and tried to talk, but at first nothing would make it past my parched throat. Her words were a mere bluff. They had to be. "I have no idea what you mean."

Spinning around, I walked to the rear of the room and the polished wood counter. The depth of shadow there afforded privacy from the open view of the window. She couldn't possibly know. Could she?

"Yes, you do. Frank was unusually drunk the other night at the Cricket, and I got him talking." Agatha followed me, and her purse dropped to the counter with an ominous thud.

Frank, the younger brother of Freddie, my husband and father of my cherished son. My thumb rubbed the thin band of gold on my left hand. It seemed a lifetime ago that we waved Frank and Freddie off to war aboard the transport ships. Only one brother had returned.

"I think it's time you left." My opinion of Agatha changed. I no longer liked her.

Unshed tears shimmered in her eyes. "I must land the lead. My life depends upon it."

Recalling happier times when we chatted during her fittings, I found a weak smile for her. "You have always shone like the brightest star, Miss Marshall. You don't need a new dress for that. I am sure they will give you the part on the strength of your talent."

She reached out and grabbed my arm. "You don't understand my situation. I'm desperate, and I'll do anything to get out of this mess. Stick with me, Grace, and once I'm a star, I will shower you with money. You could be my personal designer in America and all the other starlets will beg for you to dress them, too."

As soon as her fingers touched my skin, a memory thrust itself into my mind. As a child, the things I saw as waking dreams confused me. Dad explained it was a gift that came from his side of the family, but that some people wouldn't understand. Over time, I learned to bite my tongue when the scenes pulled from another person's mind didn't match their words. Or sometimes the images were so violent or upsetting, I had to escape into a piece of handwork to calm my thoughts.

My workroom disappeared, replaced by a lush drawing room I didn't recognise.

A man cloaked in shadow raised his arm and pointed at Agatha, as he yelled. "If I don't get what I want, then neither will you!"

Anxiety surged up Agatha's throat. "Everything will go our way. You'll see. Just as soon as I land this role, everything will fall into place."

I broke contact and peeled her fingers off my arm. The fight in my mind dissolved like ocean mist. A small amount of compassion crept into my soul for the other woman. Her behaviour was so out of character and different to her usual light-hearted banter. We all carried scars no one else could see, but one of Agatha's had been opened recently and drove her desperate comments.

Desperate people did desperate things. That was something else my dad used to mutter. My world would collapse if people knew the dark secret carved in my heart. My concern was not solely for myself, but to protect another. Agatha might be bluffing, but it wasn't a bluff I could afford to call.

"I have a gown I might be able to modify in time." In the storeroom was a gown I made a season ago. The customer had changed her mind about it at the last minute and, in a fit of guilt, paid for the dress but told me to keep it. The hemline was far too long to be fashionable in 1920, but there was sufficient length and fullness to both shorten and stagger it in the latest handkerchief style.

Agatha gasped back her tears and threw her arms around me. "You won't regret this. I promise. I shall pay you double what I owe, just as soon as I have the part."

"If you return here before the party tonight, we shall see what we can do." I would settle for being paid. Bringing my nerves back under control, I opened the front door and glared at the crowd. Men shuffled their feet and women looked away as they continued about their business.

"Thank you, Grace. You are a darling, and I would never intentionally tell a soul about your secret." That would have to suffice as an apology for her blackmailing me. Then clutching her bag, she hurried up the lane towards the steps and the street beyond.

"No rest for the wicked," I muttered.

Chapter Two

MY space included a storeroom, where expensive fabrics were stored away from any stray sunlight, and commissions waiting to be delivered. On a shelf and stowed in a basket, I pulled out the gown in question. A peacock blue silk composed of a simple drape; it would need the back altered as well as the hem. A sigh escaped my lips. The smiling showgirl had coerced me into working for free. There was no doubt in my mind that even if Agatha secured the starring role she sought, her faulty memory would forget all about her promise to pay me double.

"You're a fool, Grace Sullivan." My married surname wouldn't cross my lips as I reminded myself of another foolish decision made years earlier. When Dad found out that I was working for free, he'd shake his head and tell me I was far too nice and accommodating. Try as I might, I simply couldn't be any other way. But it was a lesson life seemed determined to try to drum into me.

From a locked drawer, I retrieved my notebook where I detailed clients' measurements. Then I wheeled a nude dress form over to the cutting table. I adjusted the notches in the form to Agatha's measurements before I clothed the legless and headless figure in the gown. Before I doubted myself, I took up my shears and slit the back of the gown open. A few smaller cuts and some tucks, and the sides were pinned to reveal a daring amount of spine. Perfect for a long necklace worn backwards to dangle against her skin.

Time lost all meaning around me as I considered the drape of the fabric and the final effect. My hands snipped, tucked, and pinned. My knees ached when Sam, my best friend in the entire world, entered the shop two hours later. Beside her, the small dark-haired boy who was the centre of my world.

I held out my arms, and Theo rushed towards me. "We're making a kite. Can we fly it in the gardens at the weekend?" he said.

"Of course we can." I kissed his cheek.

Samantha Kostas, or Sam as she preferred, ran her family bakery, starting her day at a time most of us called *the dead of night*. That meant she finished early, collected Theo from the childminder, and walked him home for me. I couldn't have raised my son without the support of my dad and best friend. Between us all, we might see him become a fine young man one day. Even if his features made my heart ache for his resemblance to his father, with the small cleft in his chin and laughing amber eyes. At least he didn't have his father's burnished copper hair, but instead, he had inherited the Sullivan family's dark locks.

I patted my son's unruly hair, which seemed determined to point upwards once his cap was removed. "Can you tell Dad I have to work late? A client wants this finished for a party tonight."

Sam screwed up her face. "You shouldn't be walking home at night alone. I'll ask Joseph to come fetch you. He can bring that horrid contraption he loves so much."

Joseph was my cousin, and he now boarded in Ascot Street, close to us. Once he had been a joyful lad, whom my dad referred to as *wet behind the ears*. Like many of our young men, he had signed up as soon as he was old enough for the grand adventure of going off to war. None of us knew the horrors he endured. Joseph returned to us with a haunted look in his eyes and his easy smile had been erased forever. Or so it seemed.

He was a policeman by day but helped Dad in the evenings if he needed two feet. Since Dad only had one. Both men delighted in tinkering with greasy motors, and Theo loved being part of *man time*, as we called it, when the three of them sat out in Dad's workshop and garage.

"Thanks, Sam. I'll eat when I get home." I kissed Theo's cheek and hugged my friend.

"You're too thin. I'll make sure there's enough left

over for you and mind you eat it before going to bed." She waggled a finger at me.

I worked all afternoon and when the light faded, I flicked the light switch (offering a silent thanks to Mrs Cooper for installing electricity throughout the building) and kept working. The seams weren't as perfect as I'd like them, and there had been no time to hand sew them all. My reliable Singer had valiantly tackled the staggered hem and the additional fabric I added to drape beautifully around Agatha's long legs. The scandalous back had a single drape of vibrant chiffon running down one side in a peacock pattern with a beaded edge, and that trailed behind in a modern twist on the form and train of a gown from before the war.

By the time Agatha pushed through the door again, my fingers hurt, my back ached, and I had stabbed myself at least three times. Would she appreciate I literally bled for her to finish on time? Probably not. I helped her dress in the fitting room with walls covered in the strawberry thief wallpaper pattern by William and Morris. The cheeky bird about to feast on a fat strawberry reminded me of the fantails that flitted around our place.

Agatha spun before the full-length mirror, and the silk flowed like water with her movement. "It's beautiful. You don't know what this means to me." Her hands shook as she let the fabric slide through her fingers.

It meant ten pounds to me. If she had ordered such a gown in Paris, Agatha would pay nearly one hundred pounds. Perhaps one day when I grew my fashion house to have a team of skilled seamstresses, I could command such prices. Today I'd settle for a tenth of what they charged.

"What about your dress? Do you want me to wrap it so you can take it with you?" I pointed to the dress she had worn into the fitting room.

Agatha waved her hand. "I'll collect it tomorrow. When I pay you. I absolutely pinkie swear that I'll find the money somehow." She held out one hand, her little finger crooked.

A childish gesture, but it might stick in her memory. I grasped her pinkie with mine and we shook on it.

"Now, wish me luck." She beamed at me, her eyes full of expectation and hope, but the whites showed a little too much, as though she were holding back panic.

"Knock 'em dead." I wished her well. Everybody had a dream and Agatha wanted to achieve hers. Who knew, perhaps one day I would sit in the cinema and see her dance across the screen. Even better if she wore one of my dresses and I had a fat bank account from all the lucrative commissions.

After she had left, I tidied up, then turned off the lights and locked the front door. A rumble came from Lambton Quay and a bright headlight flashed along the walkway in the fading twilight. A throaty motorcycle idled on the footpath.

"Grace?" a familiar voice called out.

"Coming!" I tugged the front of my cardigan

against the slight chill in the air and hurried down the lane.

Joseph sat astride a motorcycle. Not my preferred form of transport, but tonight all I wanted to do was kick off my shoes and fall into bed. The Triumph would soon deliver me to home—assuming my bones didn't rattle apart on the trip.

As a child, every Christmas Joseph and I were forced together when Dad and I returned to the family farm over in the Wairarapa. The years had changed my cousin and added bulk to his tall frame. While I once thought him annoying, I cried when he enlisted and shed even more tears in relief to have him home. While we often argued as family could, we looked out for one another.

War aged his eyes, like so many of our men. They walked up the gangplanks of the troopships with laughter in their hearts and returned weary old men. At least he came back to us. So many never did.

"Thanks for coming to get me, Joseph."

He shrugged. "Can't have you wandering home alone at twilight."

He held out a hand and steadied me as I hiked up my skirt and lifted a leg over the bike. Holding onto his waist, I pressed myself to his broad back and hoped my hat stayed on my head.

We roared up Lambton Quay, thankfully avoiding the tram lines that could ensnare a narrow motorcycle tire. As one, we leaned into the left-hand corner of Bowen Street. Thorndon was an odd neighbourhood with its mix of grand villas and workingmen cottages. As though the strict rules governing England were shaken free when the immigrants arrived Downunder. In our little neighbourhood, the upper crust lived close to labourers. Ascot Street was steep, like many a road around Wellington. Other bits were pedestrian access only, but no challenge for the motorcycle.

Houses were stepped up the hill. Terraces had been created to give each home a level building site. Our two-storey cottage had Dad's workshop crammed in between us and our neighbour on a lower level. On the higher side of us, lived Sam and her mum.

A light glowed in our cottage as I waved goodbye to Joseph and pushed open the door. Downstairs was the kitchen, dining room, and lounge. All were combined into one space after Dad and his ever-present hammer had taken down a wall to make the cottage feel less cramped. A small bedroom was tucked under the steep stairs and was Dad's private domain. Theo and I both had rooms upstairs, nestled under the steep roof.

Dad sat in an armchair in the corner closest to the cold fireplace, a book open on his chest. His eyelids fluttered open as I approached.

"I wasn't asleep. Just resting my eyes." He closed the book and placed it on the squat table beside him that also held an empty coffee cup.

"How was Theo this evening?" I flopped into the nearby armchair and immediately toed off my brown Oxfords.

"He helped me for a bit after dinner. We're building a birdhouse together. Then we had a story, and he went off to bed without complaint." Dad washed his hands over his face and scratched his silver hair. Despite being in his early fifties, he still possessed a good head of hair.

"Thanks, Dad." Not only did he cook dinner for his grandson and read him a story at bedtime, but he had also raised a daughter on his own. Like many Kiwi blokes, he simply got on with the job at hand. He might bluff and bluster at times like a bear with a sore head, but he has the biggest heart.

"He's a fine lad. Takes after me, obviously." Dad huffed a laugh. "Your dinner's in the oven, Sam dropped off a pie. What had you working so late?"

I padded to the kitchen in my stocking-clad feet and cracked open the old range. A plate sat within, a silver pot lid balanced on top to stop my tea from drying out.

"Agatha Marshall wanted a gown at very short notice. She has some fancy party tonight at Antrim House." Using a tea towel to protect my hands, I pulled out the plate and set it on the pine table. Lifting the lid, I sniffed the meal. A slice of chicken pie, a baked spud, and a handful of beans awaited me. The golden pastry of the pie and delicious aroma could only have been crafted by Sam. While both Dad and I relied on our hands to earn a living, neither of us had mastered cooking. We survived with the handful of meals we could reliably produce without burning, but Sam supplemented our diet with a range of pies, casseroles, and cakes.

"Is she the one who never pays?" Dad grabbed his empty cup and carried it over to the sink.

"That's her." I shovelled pie into my face so I could claim chewing as an excuse for not continuing that conversation.

I mouthed the next words out of his mouth along with dad. "You're too good, Grace."

Exactly what I knew he'd say when he found out that yet again, Agatha had skipped out of my shop without paying. I stabbed a chunk of potato and nodded. The food chilled as it hit my stomach. *You're too good.* But I wasn't. That was my secret that Frank must have shared with Agatha.

"I know, Dad. But she convinced me it was a matter of life or death." Or a matter of secrets or silence.

Dad blew a snort. "She won't die if she wears a dress everyone has seen before. Any customer with an outstanding bill who comes here wanting work is told to bugger off. I don't suppose you asked her for payment upfront?" Dad grabbed a tea towel as I turned on the tap and let hot water flow into the sink.

I reached for the Sunlight soap, held in a metal cage with a handle and agitated the water with the contraption.

"Oh, Grace," Dad said when I remained silent.

"She said if she made it big, she would shower me with money." I tried not to cry and kept my gaze fixed on the soapy water. The image of a red bicycle appeared in my mind, and then it shimmered and dissolved like a soap bubble.

"We're a right pair, aren't we?" He nudged me with his shoulder.

I balanced the soap holder above the taps to drain. Then I flung my arms around him. "We'll make do, just like we always have. The three of us against the world."

Dad thumped me on the back. "Things are looking up now, love. You wait and see. The bad times are behind us and everything is turning bright. Your business will take off, and you'll soon need to take on more seamstresses."

Dad was right. Again. The world had climbed out of the trenches of the Great War only to plunge into plague pits. Influenza spread through communities and seemed to select its victims at random. It might be one soul from a family or the entire lot. We were blessedly unscathed. Dad caught it, but I nursed him through. Sam lost her dad, and we buried him along with so many others.

"There does seem to be a wind of change in the air. Like the burst of spring after a long winter." I saw it reflected in fashion magazines. Hems became shorter, colours more vibrant, and embellishments shinier. The music emerging from America had a faster tempo to match. If I could capture the wave, it might sweep our family into prosperity. All I needed was the courage to grasp the electricity shooting from the new trends and put a unique Kiwi twist on them.

After we had done the dishes, I sat with Dad for a

while until he muttered his goodnight and stomped off to his room. I tried to read, but the words swam on the page. My shoes dangled from one hand as I trod the stairs and peered into Theo's room. My son slept with his teddy bear clutched to his chest and his mouth open in a gentle snore. The sight made my heart swell.

I kept my door ajar, in case Theo needed me during the night, and quickly stripped off my dress and slipped on a nightgown. Once in bed, I stretched out and wriggled my toes before curling on my side and tucking the quilt around me. When sleep found me, I was dreaming of a fabulous party with fast music and women in glorious beaded gowns.

Chapter Three

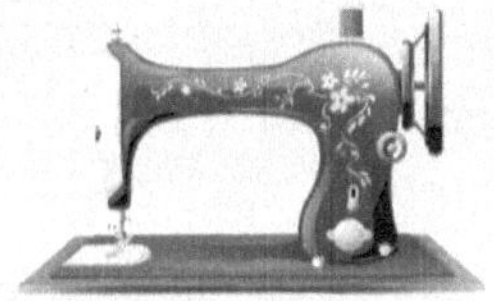

THE NEXT MORNING FOLLOWED THE SAME ROUTINE as every other day. Once up and dressed, I roused Theo and laid out his clothes for him. Being a big boy now, as he announced in a sleepy tone, he didn't need me to dress him anymore. A pang shot through my heart at the tiny tendrils of independence emerging from him. My mind baulked at imagining him a grown lad because it conjured that day at the wharf when Frank stole a kiss, and we waved as Freddie and our men chugged away to war.

I spread jam on toast for Theo before buttering my own. Dad joked as usual and asked Theo about his plans for the day.

"Come along, Theo. Go wash your face and brush your teeth and we'll head off. Poppa has work to do." I pulled his chair away from the table.

Theo heaved a sigh. "I don't want to go to Mrs Rogers. Why can't I go to school? I'm a big lad now."

"When you turn five, which is not so far away." I turned him around and pushed him in the direction of the bathroom. My boy was in such a hurry to grow up, yet I wanted to slow down time and enjoy every moment of his childhood years. Life taught me a lesson in brutality and how I longed to protect him from the horror we had seen. To let him keep his innocence a little longer.

"He's a fine lad, Grace. Stop worrying about him." Dad poured himself another mug of tea and picked up the paper.

I busied myself clearing the table and stacking our dishes by the sink to wash. Theo never knew his father. Freddie had died on a battlefield far away before the two could meet. His Uncle Frank filled the role of father and made it clear he would do so on an official basis. If only I would have him.

But something gave me pause. My life was full enough with Theo, Dad, and building my business. If I admitted my selfishness, I didn't want to put my dreams aside and have to tend to a husband. Nor did I intend to hand over my earnings to someone else. I worked hard to establish myself as a seamstress, and I aspired to one day run my own fashion house. To have women vie to attend my showings and to have a bookings ledger overflowing with wealthy women and starlets eager to wear one of *Grace Designs*.

Besides, I didn't love Frank. Sure, I liked him and enjoyed his company, but never again would I be so carefree with my heart. His brother taught me that lesson well. There was another, darker reason that nibbled at me. One that made a shadow cross my vision at times when I touched Frank. What secrets did he hide from me?

After breakfast, Theo took my hand for the walk to Mrs Rogers, who lived on The Terrace. Once he had dashed off to play in her small rear garden with the other children she minded, I headed down Plimmer Steps and opened up my shop. The postie had been by early, and I swept up the letters pushed through the brass slot, while idly wondering if Agatha had secured the role she wanted. Flashes of her memory raced through my mind. Had everything fallen into place for her and the angry man?

Standing behind the counter, I opened mail and sorted invoices that needed paying into one pile and the rest into another. The bell tinkled as Etty entered on the dot of nine.

"Good morning. How are you feeling today?" I scanned her face for a dripping nose but found only a slight redness.

Etty was a petite wee thing, with masses of red hair courtesy of her Irish blood, and a fiery temper to match. She also made an impeccable stitch and followed instructions to the letter. If there was a way to duplicate the hard worker, I could take on more commissions or even make my own ready-to-wear line.

"Much better, thank you, Mrs Devine." Etty stripped off her gloves and hat and stored them under the counter.

"How many times must I ask you to call me Grace?" It amused me how Etty held to the rigid formality of a department store. I was certainly no better than her, and New Zealand had established itself to be free of England's strict social hierarchy. Here, anything was possible. A shopgirl could reach for the moon. If she dared.

"It doesn't feel right, though. You're my employer." Etty pulled a cloth from under the counter and wiped the glass surface free of any fingerprints.

"But we are also friends, are we not?" Not the tight friendship I had with Sam, but I worked alongside Etty most days. We knew the details of each other's lives and with that came a certain level of camaraderie.

She rubbed harder at a stubborn mark. "Of course, but I am still going to call you Mrs Devine. Now, what shall I tackle today?"

I really wished she wouldn't call me that. By instinct, I rubbed the band on my finger and suppressed a grimace, replacing it with a weak smile. Etty might be short of stature, but she was immovable when she dug her toes in. "We have two fittings today. One is for a hem for Miss Field on her walking suit. The other is the first fitting for Miss Howell. Can you make sure the teal silk is ready for her?"

"Of course," Etty murmured.

We would place the gown on a dress form, so the client's first look gave her a better idea of how it would drape on her body. Then the excitement built as we removed it from the headless shape and lowered it onto the client as she watched in the mirror.

The day passed smoothly. My client even paid her account in full before taking the walking suit with her, carefully wrapped in brown paper after Etty had finished the hem. As she left, I peered up and down the lane, hoping to see Agatha's face as she waved a fistful of cash at me. No such luck.

With a productive day behind us, I closed up early that Friday afternoon. The first fitting had left, and we had pinned the gown for alteration next week. Two more outfits had their pieces cut out and were waiting in a flat pile to be started. Etty and I chatted about our plans for the weekend before we parted ways. Sam and I planned to see a picture on Saturday night, and I had promised to take Theo to fly his kite in the Botanic Gardens, confident that windy Wellington would provide the gusts he needed.

At home, Dad and Theo worked on their birdhouse, which resembled a villa with a porch out front and fretwork over the veranda. I should have known my woodworker father was incapable of a simple, unadorned, square birdhouse. Leaving the men to their task, I set about preparing dinner. As I laid the table, I grabbed the discarded newspaper and scanned the headline. My hand froze.

Death visits Antrim House. Popular showgirl dead.

The black-and-white photograph showed a blanket-draped figure tucked beside the wall of some outbuilding, possibly the stables of Antrim House. But that wasn't the bit that arrested my movement. It was the drape of fabric that had escaped the covering. A familiar peacock pattern with a beaded fringe I had stitched only the night before and attached to a dress for a *popular showgirl*.

Agatha.

My body dropped to the chair, and I devoured the article, although it contained scant details. Early Friday morning, revellers heading home from the party had stumbled across the body.

"Oh, Agatha." Not the luck she had hoped for when she headed off to her party the night before. A part of me mourned the snuffing of a bright light, who would shine no more upon the Wellington stage. Then a tiny pragmatic voice whispered there was no chance of her bill being settled now.

Imagining the lecture from Dad, I folded up the newspaper again. He would find out soon enough. Then I would have to meet his disappointed gaze over the dinner table. While New Zealand didn't follow all of England's societal rules, etiquette said I couldn't repossess a gown from a corpse. Handing over an overdue invoice to the family at the funeral was probably also frowned upon. An expensive gown, now utterly ruined by damp grass and whatever else it had encountered from being left out overnight. Was there blood on it? The article failed to mention how the unfortunate woman had met her demise.

A sigh heaved through me. "When will you learn, Grace?" No more credit. If a client failed to pay for one outfit, they most certainly would not get another. Even if they know my secret.

Voices came from the back door, and Theo burst in with a huge smile. "Poppa let me use the hammer."

Dad ruffled Theo's dark locks. "He's not bad. Only hit my thumb twice."

I winced in sympathy with my father. "Why don't you sit down, and I'll fetch a couple of ginger beers."

Dad stomped to the armchair with his uneven gait. He had lost his right foot just above the ankle when I was a baby. Being a woodworker, he had made the replacement foot himself, carving the toes and tendons to match its companion. As a child, he told me he and his sailor mates were playing soccer with a live munition. As Dad told the story, he had given it a particularly good kick to score the winning goal when the thing had exploded taking off his foot. I didn't believe him, but he kept what really happened hidden deep inside him where even my gift couldn't reach it.

The accident resulted in him being discharged from the navy with a modest pension. Not long after, he swore off the grog entirely. For years, he had brewed ginger beer with all the attention and determination he showed to his other projects. I fetched two bottles, and we toasted each other and listened to music on the radio.

MONDAY MORNING SAW Etty and me about our business with a subdued atmosphere in the shop. Everyone talked of Agatha's tragic death and rumours ran wild as to what happened at the party that had resulted in her demise. While the papers finally revealed her identity at the weekend, they were keeping mum on exactly what happened.

As I laid out pattern pieces on the cutting table within easy reach and pinned them on a dummy, I wondered if she had wowed Liam before wandering off in the dark. Perhaps buoyed by her success, she had drunk too much and tumbled in the dark. If she landed on her back and became sick, there would have been no one to roll her to her side and ensure her throat remained clear.

The bell rang and a heavier tread than usual entered my workroom. With a back piece in my hand, I turned and nearly swallowed my mouthful of pins. A man stood on the threshold. Of average height, his broad shoulders filled his grey suit jacket in a way that made me admire the cut of the garment and assume it was tailored and not off the rack.

With one hand, he removed his fedora to reveal thick black hair, trimmed short—most likely in an effort to keep the curl under control. Or it might be the haircut of a man who retained some habits from time served in the military. Dark eyes regarded me from a square face with a dark cast to it. New Zealand was a melting pot of nationalities and his heritage could have harked back to Italy, Greece, or the Middle East.

Except he walked into my shop with a coiled tension about him, like a warrior about to confront an invading British soldier. Or a panther moving through the trees, stalking its prey. Yet he also possessed a quiet dignity that hinted at Maori blood coursing through his veins.

He nodded in my direction and walked farther into the shop. "Good morning. I'm Detective Archer and I'm investigating the death of Miss Marshall and need to speak with Mrs Devine."

"That's me," I spoke around the pins, then removed them from between my teeth and shoved them into the cushion tied at my wrist. "I saw the news in the paper. How terrible. She was in such high spirits when I last saw her."

He tossed his hat to the counter and surveyed the workroom. Then his calm gaze settled on me. "That's why I'm here. You seem to be the last person who saw her alive."

A retort surged through me. "Impossible! She was on her way to that party, and I am sure most of Wellington saw her at Antrim House. Agatha was hard to miss, always so bright and beautiful."

"She never made it to the party." His attention never wavered from my face.

It unnerved me, as though he stared through to my soul and would pluck out any secret I tried to hide. My mind tried to reconcile what he told me with my memory of that evening. "How can that be? She came here for final adjustments to her dress and left to head straight to the party." It wasn't like she could get lost on the way. Antrim House was visible from the top of Plimmer Steps and was within what the lads would call *spitting distance*.

"Did she?" He splayed one hand over the smooth glass of the counter. Underneath I had an array of embellishments and embroidered pieces women could choose for their outfits. His hand sat above a butterfly that could anchor a series of gathers.

His words dripped through me and spread a chill through my limbs. "I don't understand what you are getting at, Detective." I let go of the piece of fabric and it dangled from the sole pin securing it to the shoulder of the form.

He gestured to the leather armchair. "Why don't you sit down, Mrs Devine, and tell me everything that happened when you last saw Miss Marshall?"

I'd rather not sit and have him looming over me. Instead, I clasped my hands together to stop the shake and tried to meet his stare. "I'd rather stand, thank you, as there is very little to tell. I altered a gown for Miss Marshall. She came here on her way to the party. I dressed her, made a few final touches, we chatted, and she left."

"What did you talk about?" He spoke in a low tone, never raising his voice or rushing.

I suspected nothing on earth could ruffle his feathers. If we had been deep in a trench about to go over the top, he would have relayed commands in the same calm voice.

"Miss Marshall was excited about a new show

being put on at the Cricket. Apparently, some Holly-wood producer is in New Zealand and is rumoured to be attending when it opens. She thought it might be her big break." I didn't see how the chatter of two women in a fitting room had any bearing on her death. Telling the detective of Agatha's dreams sat uneasily within me. It violated her confidence. While a seamstress didn't have the same vow of confidentiality as a priest, surely it was implied when women were in such an intimate setting. A woman was literally exposed and stripped bare, as I pinned fabric to create a new look.

"How long was she here?" He leaned back against the counter, fingers curled around the glass edge.

"An hour or two, as I had to stitch the hem at the right length." I fidgeted with the pin cushion. His quiet questions made words bubble inside me wanting to burst free and fill the silence he let fall between us. How many tiny glass-headed pieces of metal would I need to seal my lips, to keep my secrets from spilling out?

Chapter Four

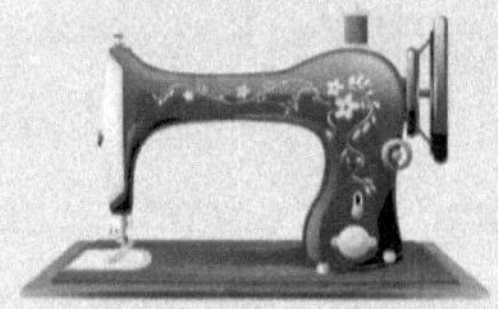

Detective Archer relieved me of his piercing gaze and glanced at Etty, who kept her head down as she sewed at a smaller table in the back of the room. "Who came in with Miss Marshall?"

"No one. We were alone." That day played over and over in my head. Her heated words flung in anger, the hushed tones tinged with desperation. What had happened to Agatha at the party? I struggled to believe the detective, that she never made it to the event. That meant no one had seen how marvellous she looked in the dress. What a waste of my time and effort.

"Which way did she go when she left?" He pulled a notebook from his jacket pocket and a pencil scratched over a page as he recorded my answers.

"She went up the lane, of course. Antrim House is a mere five minutes from here." In my mind, I saw Agatha wave farewell and then turn to her left as she exited my shop.

"Did you follow her?" he asked in a soft tone.

I glanced up and narrowed my gaze. What an odd question. Why on earth would I wander out in the fading light after her? "Of course not. I had to close up here and wanted to get home to my dinner and bed."

"Miss Marshall was discovered by the old stables of Antrim House, she never entered the house. Did she mention meeting anyone there?" His gaze pinned me to the spot like a piece of fabric on the dress form.

Why would she stop at the stables before entering the party? To meet a friend, perhaps, or a quick swig from a flask for courage? Anything I could suggest as to what ran through her mind that night would be a stab in the dark. "Agatha chatted about the Hollywood producer and the movies he has made."

"Why would she go through the stables and not up the path to Antrim House?" More questions swirled in his dark eyes.

Why did Agatha do anything? Opposite Plimmer Steps, Boulcott Street made a ninety-degree turn before running up to meet The Terrace. Antrim House nestled in that block, surrounded by its laid-out grounds. A modest villa sat on the very corner across from the steps, the Italianate mansion visible behind it. "Agatha was all about the direct approach. I suspect she stood on the top step, locked her gaze on the house and walked in a straight line, rather than along the path to the main entrance."

"Did anyone see you leave here?" The question hung heavy in the air. The implication was that he doubted my version of events and expected me to provide a witness.

Luckily, I could provide one who could not be doubted. A member of his own police force. "Yes. Joseph Sullivan collected me on his motorcycle and delivered me to my doorstep. He's a policeman."

That made one eyebrow quirk, but it quickly fell back into line with its mate. "Constable Sullivan?"

"That's him." I suppose there could be other Joseph Sullivans who were policemen in Wellington, but how many also possessed a bone-jarring motorcycle?

His eyes narrowed. "Are you...involved with him?"

Laughter burst from my chest. If the pins had still been clutched between my teeth, they would have shot at the detective like tiny darts. It took some effort to swallow the fit the ludicrous idea induced. "Not likely. He's my cousin."

Again the heavy, silent stare. Then he dropped his gaze and there was more scratching before the detective closed the notebook and tucked it into his jacket pocket. "I may have more questions for you, Mrs Devine."

I didn't like him. Something in his manner bristled over my skin and set my teeth to aching. And yet he had been perfectly polite, and his tone remained quiet throughout. It was his eyes that undid me. As though he saw every secret running under my skin that I tried to keep hidden.

Needing to move, I strode to the door and flung it open a little too vigorously. The bell clanged like an alarm and took several seconds to settle. Etty startled and dropped the skirt she worked on.

Detective Archer picked up his fedora and placed it on his head at a slight angle. The smallest flash of a smile shimmered in his eyes, then it faded away. He nodded and walked from my shop, and I hoped, my life.

Etty stared out the window as the policeman walked back down the lane. "Detectives don't investigate accidents, do they?"

Only then did I realise the detective never said outright that Agatha had met a foul end. But his visit certainly implied it. Nor had the newspapers mentioned anything other than her name and that she had died unexpectedly sometime on Thursday night.

"I don't know Etty. Perhaps it is merely a formality when a young person dies suddenly?" But exactly how did Agatha die? Healthy young people didn't usually drop dead for no reason. Not now both the Great War and the Spanish Flu were behind us. Agatha had stood in my room not long before her death and she seemed in fine mettle to me.

"Maybe it was her heart? That can take anyone at any time, and you never know when it's simply going to stop." Etty offered helpful suggestions of ways a person might meet a sudden and unexpected end.

I didn't want to contemplate the many ways a person could die. Not after we had lost millions in a few dark years. Time for a brighter and more hopeful topic. "Shall we pull out the trimmings and see what colour will go with the peach linen? I was thinking a very pale green."

We soon forgot the disruption to our day caused by the detective's visit. By late afternoon, Etty and I had achieved a satisfying amount. I had two dresses cut out for a small collection of ready-to-wear clothing I intended to display in my window. If that proved successful, more would follow.

Etty emerged from the fitting room with a yellow and white dress in her hands. "Who does this belong to? It's not one of ours, and I found it tucked in the corner of the shelf."

I stared at the dress, an off-the-rack number from Kirkcaldie and Stains. A hurried conversation about the item slowly dripped into my brain. "Oh, my goodness. It's the one Miss Marshall was wearing Thursday evening. She meant to collect it Friday."

My assistant frowned at the dress and held it at arm's length as though its owner's untimely death cont-aminated it. "Do we give it to her family or the police?"

There was a question I never had to contemplate before. "I don't know, Etty. I'll wrap it up and ask Joseph. Although I'm sure delivering it to her family would be the right thing to do. It's not like a forgotten day dress is evidence of a crime." Some garments were fashion crimes, but police didn't meddle in fabrics. And the dress was rather stylish.

I took the dress from her and shook it out to release some wrinkles. A soft pop caught my attention and, glancing down, a folded piece of paper had shaken loose from the fabric. I picked it up and opened the square that revealed an old newspaper article. '*Tragedy snatches life of schoolgirl*', read the headline. A quick scan detailed the accidental death of a girl at the local private school. Horrible, but tragic. Why would Agatha have it tucked in her dress? A friend perhaps, the date was ten years ago, and they might have been at school together. The article might have been a sentimental token. I slid the article into my apron pocket.

Returning my attention to the dress, I spread it out on the cutting table. A long habit of working in the department store made my hands smooth the wrinkles, ensuring it was flat before folding it over a piece of tissue paper. My fingers skimmed the material, searching for any pockets or other hidden items.

As a woman and a seamstress, I had mixed feelings about pockets. As a woman, I wanted pockets large enough to hold a handkerchief, a small sewing kit, and a sandwich. As a designer, I knew that as soon as you added pockets, women would shove far too much in them and ruin the lines of a dress. Thankfully we had aprons with their voluminous pockets for around the workroom and at home.

Next, I fetched a sheet of thick brown paper and wrapped the folded dress. In pen, I added—*property of Miss Agatha Marshall*—in a neat hand, before placing the parcel on a shelf in the storage room. As I locked up the workroom and waved goodbye to Etty, Frank waited in the lane. He pushed off the wall where he had been lounging and stepped to my side.

"Frank, what brings you this way?" I took my brother-in-law's offered arm. Tall and lanky, he had returned from the war with what some women called an appealingly rough edge. A darkness simmered in his amber eyes that some found irresistible. Whereas the shadows edging his life gave me pause. Or perhaps it was merely his similarity to his brother. Only a year had separated Freddie and Frank, and in appearance, they could almost pass for twins.

"Do I need a reason to see you, Grace?" he asked.

When I stared at him, he shrugged. "Heard that detective was sniffing around here today. I wanted to make sure everything was all right."

No surprise that Frank knew about my unannounced visitor. He had a sixth sense when it came to the boys in blue—so he could avoid them. The only time I ever saw Frank in the same room as a copper was when both he and Joseph attended Theo's birthday parties.

"He was asking about Agatha Marshall. She came here before she ran off to her party." A Cinderella in a borrowed gown, who never made it to the ball. Now the authorities cast suspicious eyes on the fairy godmother who clothed her. "Do you know what happened to her?" Part of me was morbidly curious. As Etty rightly observed, healthy young people don't usually drop dead without a push from either war or disease. Another part of me shivered from a chilly warning that whatever happened, it was nothing good.

"Word is she was murdered." He shot me a look as he said the last word.

"Gosh." Murdered? How...dramatic. It certainly ensured her spot on the front page of the news. Agatha's ghost was probably chuffed to bits.

"The gardener for Antrim House found her body and reckons she'd been smacked in the head." He took the road side of the footpath and that let me stare into shop windows as we walked up the road.

"That doesn't mean murder though, does it? Perhaps she fell and hit her head on something?" Like the schoolgirl in the old article, who died in a similar way. I couldn't believe anyone would want to harm the showgirl. Even if she ran up debts she never intended to pay and threatened to blackmail people.

Frank's lips quirked. "People don't usually fall and hit their head more than once on a shovel."

Oh. That was horrid.

"If that copper gives you any trouble, you let me know and I'll deal with it." Frank kept his eyes straight ahead as he made the offer. A tightness in his jaw and shoulders left little doubt as to *how* he would deal with the detective.

A shiver ran down my spine. The world had seen too much death and violence. Now was a time for peace and healing. "Leave him be, Frank. I'm sure I'll never see him again. Not unless he is seized by a sudden desire for a couture gown."

The tension in his body evaporated and he flashed

me a grin. "He might want something pretty for the policeman's ball."

"In that case, I would only be too happy to design something fabulous. Although I might charge a little more than usual for the extra fabric." The idea of taking the detective's measurements in my fitting room as he stood in his socks and underpants caused a sudden lurch in my stomach. Best not to dwell on that.

I leaned into Frank's side. We had our ups and downs, but he was family and there was a comfort in the company of someone who shared our hardships. Thinking about my history with Frank reminded me that he had put me in a pickle by over-sharing certain aspects of our past. But how to broach the subject?

We walked on in silence until Frank cast me a sideways glance. "What are you chewing over in that mind, Grace? Your lips keep moving, but nothing is coming out."

Sometimes, I rehearsed what to say in my head, unaware that my body mouthed the words, testing the feel of them over my tongue before I gave them voice. "That day, Agatha said something that made me feel I had to alter the dress for her."

Worry gnawed at me. If Agatha knew, what if she had told someone else or written it down? In my mind, I imagine my secret scrawled in scarlet lipstick on a mirror for all to see. Then I wondered, what other secrets had Agatha been ferreting out?

"Oh?" Frank shouldered a man out of the way who barrelled down the path without looking.

"She said she knew a secret about me," I muttered the words out the side of my mouth, not daring to say them too loud when anyone might hear on the busy street. Now that the moment came to confront Frank, I struggled to accuse him. He was fiercely protective of Theo and me, and I knew he wouldn't do anything to hurt us.

He scratched his jaw, the stubble breaking through the surface of his skin as the day lengthened. "You know what she was like, hardly the deepest puddle in the street. She would have been just taking a punt to rattle you and get what she wanted."

"She seemed awfully sure she knew something that I would want to be kept quiet." My hands curled. I would protect what was mine. If I had to. Not that I knew how, but Dad and Mrs Cooper always said I could do anything if I put my mind to it.

Frank laughed. "She could turn on the charm, that one. Had a way of getting you to open up so she could scratch out any juicy titbits for her own entertainment. Even if she knew something, what does it matter now? She took whatever it might have been to her grave."

I could only hope that was the case. Perhaps Frank was right. Agatha was a delightful and entertaining client, and I could imagine people telling her more than they meant to. She might have merely thrown the accusation and hoped she struck a chord within me. Her tactic had worked, and I had laboured all day to alter the gown for her.

Frank walked with me until we reached the intersection of The Terrace and Bowen Street. His black Ford Model T was parked on the side of the road.

We stopped to say our goodbyes, and he kept hold of my hand. "If you're not doing anything later this week, I'd like to take you out, Grace. How about dinner and a movie?"

I loved going to the picture theatre with its orchestra down in front and the chance to scrutinise what everyone wore both on the screen and in the audience. Agatha might have dreamed of starring in pictures, I simply loved watching them and letting myself get carried away in the story. An evening out might provide the distraction I needed. "Thursday?"

A lopsided grin tugged one corner of his lips, then he bent his head to kiss my cheek. "Thursday it is."

Chapter Five

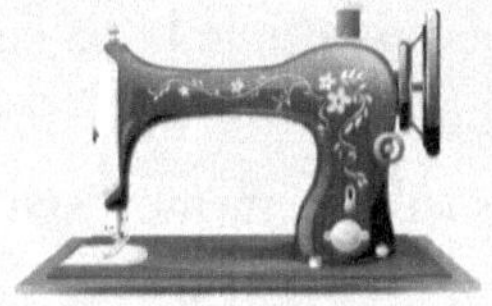

Two days later on Wednesday, as the notorious Wellington wind tried to strip hats from heads and even unbutton coats from bodies, we gathered to farewell Agatha. Despite the summer warmth in the air, few people loitered outside due to the chill bite of the wind and we sought sanctuary from the weather inside.

Sam insisted on accompanying me so that, in her words, I didn't face the gossips alone after the detective's visit. Not that I had anything to be concerned about or to hide. The policeman's questions were only a formality, and it was his job to try to find out what had happened to Miss Marshall. I had grilled Joseph for more information about how Agatha had died, and my quiet cousin only relented when I said I already knew it was murder. He then let slip that the detective had questioned him about if he had taken me home and if he had seen me leaving the shop or coming back down the steps. He even asked if Joseph had seen Agatha leave my shop, to which he truthfully replied he had not.

That answer took up residence in my gut like a mouldy piece of bread. Solid, uncomfortable, and emitting an unsettling trickle through my body. How rude of Detective Archer to assume I had lied. Just because a person built a better life for their family around one small untruth, doesn't mean they spoke with a forked tongue all day long.

That morning, I had dressed in the closest items in my wardrobe to mourning and donned a long narrow skirt in deep purple and a fitted jacket in purple and black. A plain black hat pinned to my hair to finish the outfit. Sam wore trousers in a dark grey and a matching waistcoat with a fedora on her cropped hair. During the war, she had adopted a man's style of dress and afterwards, never reverted to skirts or dresses. It made no difference to me what she wore or who caught her eye. I loved Sam for who she was on the inside, and I delighted in the challenge of fitting a man's style to her curvy frame.

Hushed conversations took place in the church with its white painted ceiling that seemed to soar far above our heads. The stained glass windows cast shafts of pale yellow and red light over the pews. The coffin sat on a stand in the centre of the transept, draped in white silk and covered in white daisies with bright yellow eyes. Some people approached to place a hand on it, heads bowed for a quiet moment, before dabbing at their eyes with a handkerchief and turning to find a seat.

I wasn't such a hypocrite that I would put on a sorrowful display before God and those in attendance. Agatha would have to explain her outstanding invoices to the ultimate debt collector. No one should speak ill of the dead, so I gathered up memories of a happy, giggling client who kept an amazing dream alive in her heart.

We found seats at the back and out of the way, so we could stare at those attending. It felt like half of Wellington turned out to see the dancer's last show. Or were they simply curious, wanting to hear the latest gossip about her death? After a long few days of speculation, the police had finally released the information everyone had been poised to hear—Agatha had been murdered by a person, or persons, unknown. Most likely with the shovel found nearby with blood and hair on it.

The showgirls from the Cricket were easy to spot, even devoid of their small and sparkly stage costumes. I wondered which among them was Mintie, Agatha's competition for the leading role. With their rouged cheeks and ruby lips, they clustered like exotic birds to one side. Their hats were embellished with beaded pins and their hemlines scandalously at least two inches higher than everyone else's. I made a note to suggest shorter lengths to my clients, even though they had yet to rise in the magazines. Showgirls weren't mere followers of fashion, they led it with bayonets fixed and screaming *advance!*

Agatha's family and close friends were clustered in the front few rows. Even though everyone dressed in black, the Marshalls appeared wealthier and above us in station. The women's hats were plain, but the net veils had perfect edges. Unlike the slightly uneven line on the veils of the showgirls as though they had cut and trimmed their hats themselves. The upper-class clothing sported a minimum of embroidery and yet the cut and fit screamed of expensive restraint to my eye.

The reverend walked to the front of the church, and a hush fell over everyone. The service gave the details of Agatha's life that her family wanted to broadcast. Her work at the Cricket blurred over and reduced to a mention of her love for dancing and music. A woman, introduced as Lynn Young and a close friend of Agatha's, gave a reading.

More people used the opportunity to stand up and read a poem or recite the lyrics to one of Agatha's favourite songs. When the reverend asked us all to stand for the next psalm, a greater urge took hold of me.

"I have to use the loo," I whispered in Sam's ear. Then I darted out the side to the small bathroom off the narthex.

Within, Lynn, who had made the first reading, leaned against the wall and on seeing me, slid something behind her back.

"Oh, I'm sorry. I didn't want to intrude," I said out loud while willing my bladder to hold on a bit longer.

"Don't mind me." She waved to the only toilet in the cramped space.

My body didn't need to be told twice. When I emerged from the stall afterwards, Miss Young was still there fixing her makeup. We danced around each other at the basin. My hand grazed hers for a mere instant. A woman's voice cried inside my head, *no, no, no, not again!* It was such a plaintive cry that I wondered what had so upset her. Then I scrubbed the foreign memory away as I washed my hands.

"I don't recognise you. Are you a showgirl or a friend of Agatha's?" she asked as she flipped her compact shut and shoved it back into her handbag. A silver glint bounced from a square and slim object in her bag.

"Neither. I am Grace Devine and I made some of her outfits." I shook my hands of excess water before reaching for the towel.

"Ah. Yes. She spoke of you. Kept urging me to go see you. But I'm not as flush as Agatha, and I buy my clothes off the rack." She swept a hand down her dress and toppled slightly to one side. A faint whiff of sweet alcohol accompanied her words. I suspected she had snuck into the toilet for a quiet swig from the hip flask in her bag.

"You look lovely. I am sorry you lost your best friend." If some horrid event snatched Sam from me, I think it would take more than a few gulps from a hidden flask to fortify me. A bath full of the stuff wouldn't be enough to soothe my grief.

She huffed, and the noise sounded more laugh than a sob of grief. "Agatha was always in the spotlight. Even in death, she found a way to keep me in the shadows. My engagement to Johnny was supposed to be announced last week, but her murder has occupied the front page for days, so we had to postpone our bit of news."

Did one apologise for that? It must have been the combination of grief and liquor that made her sound bitter. Or more likely, my bad experience with Agatha over the last weeks coloured my memory of a woman whose bright smile embodied the daisies on her coffin.

"I'm sure she was an amazing friend." It seemed a bit harsh to blame Agatha for being murdered at the same time as her friend got engaged.

"Oh, Aggie was amazing all around. Top of the class at school, captain of the hockey team, had the most handsome lads running after her, and was about to become a movie star. She certainly knew how to get what she wanted." Lynn's voice was tinged with sarcasm and bitterness.

Well, when she put it that way, why on earth were the two women friends? "It could not have been all bad. You were her dearest friend after all."

A scowl flashed across her face, and before she could answer, the door handle rattled.

A square male face with a Roman nose peered in with his eyes closed, in case he saw something in the ladies he shouldn't. "Lynn? Is everything all right? The show is nearly over," he whispered.

With a nod to Miss Young, I slipped past him. Returning to my seat as the service ended, my thoughts swirling with the differences between Agatha's relationship with her best friend and mine with Sam. We would do anything for each other and celebrated the highs of life and propped each other up in the dark days.

The reverend lead the last prayer and then stepped aside for Agatha's parents to receive people. Only the family would follow the hearse to her final resting place, then there would be a private wake at the Marshall residence for a select few. Showgirls and work girls were not invited, nor were the many spectators. The older couple stood by the coffin to give mourners the opportunity to move forwards for a few quiet words, the shake of a hand, or a consoling pat on the shoulder.

"Shall we leave?" Sam murmured in my ear.

"I think we have to wait until the coffin goes past." This was my first society funeral. When we lost so many to influenza, funerals were hurried affairs with only the closest family present. Some had no one there at all. The scale of loss had overwhelmed everyone on the heels of war.

We stood by the double doors that led to the narthex and waited. The assembled people parted as Mrs Marshall made her way down the nave. Somewhere in her fifties with deep wrinkles dragging her lower eyelids farther south, she wore a black crepe suit and a tight black cloche with a single curling black feather.

She paused to talk to someone who pointed in my direction, then she advanced.

The mouldy-knot-of-bread dread in my stomach let out a grumble.

The bereaved mother halted in front of me. "Mrs Devine, I am given to understand you were the last person to see my daughter alive."

I opened my mouth to retort, no, I was the second to last person to see her. Since surely whoever did the deed was the last person to encounter her alive. "I saw Miss Marshall that evening, yes. She had a fitting on my premises, as I had finished a gown at very short notice for her. She left my shop in a fine mood and was looking forwards to the party."

"The detective has confirmed that you were the last person to see my darling girl. I wonder at your impertinence to show your face here." She dabbed at her eyes with a brilliant white handkerchief.

Mrs Marshall may as well have pointed a finger at my head and shrieked MURDERER! given how those around me reacted. Some gasped, others sucked in their breath. It was funny how some people breathed out, others in, on hearing something shocking. I froze. Sam took my hand and made a noise like the low warning growl of a small dog who packed a powerful bite.

"Detective Archer is mistaken. After farewelling Miss Marshall, I shut up my shop and left in the company of my cousin, *Constable* Sullivan." I made sure they all heard me. Sam squeezed my fingers in support.

Mrs Marshall stared at me for a long moment and seemed on the verge of hurling more accusations.

Then her husband took her arm. "It's time, Marjory, and this is not the place," he murmured.

Remembering her stiff-British upper lip, Mrs Marshall gave a curt nod and spun on her expensive heels to walk back to her daughter. The pallbearers stepped forwards and lifted the flower-draped coffin, careful not to disturb the floral tributes. With slow steps and solemn expressions, they carried the coffin down the nave, her family falling into step behind.

Once they had passed through the doors, louder conversation broke out and I let out a long breath of relief.

"Come on, let's head home. We could both do with a cup of tea after that." Sam took my arm.

As we left the church, I spotted Mrs Cooper holding court under the shelter of a stout tree with a distinct southerly lean to one side. Clad in an impeccable black suit I had made for her the previous year, when she announced she wanted something *fashionable* for the funerals her position meant she attended. Her hat harked back to a previous era and was a daring move. Not because it was out of fashion for such a maven, but because the full brim was a taunt to the wind.

I approached when the couple conversing with her

was dismissed. "Hello, Mrs Cooper. I wasn't aware you knew Miss Marshall?"

"I knew of her but did not know her. I am acquainted with her family. They are old stock, you know. The Marshalls came over on the Aurora in 1840 and consider themselves the leading family of Wellington society. Apparently, no one told them this isn't America with its deference to its founding families," she spoke in a low tone.

"It is a tragedy, what happened. I am sure Miss Marshall will be sorely missed by her family." Another tragedy was the rather large and unpaid account she left behind. Then I berated myself for being a horrid person, to think of money at such a time.

"I'm not so sure about that," Mrs Cooper murmured.

I glanced up sharply. "Oh?" How could a vibrant young person like Miss Marshall not be missed by those who knew and loved her?

"Some will mutter that a dark blot on the family name has been expunged. It was a bit of a shock to them when she declared her intention of being a showgirl, rather than a wife and mother. That set isn't considered acceptable to attend our soirees, even though the gentlemen delight in their company. Actually, that's probably why the wives and mothers don't like them." Mrs Cooper winked at me.

The grand dame had a worldly view, but I wondered if Mr Cooper had ever showered a pretty young thing in jewels and money. Probably not. I don't think he would ever have dared. Sam and I suppressed our laughter. It wasn't hard to see why the gorgeous showgirls and men with spare cash were a match the social set would rather keep apart.

"There are also rumours of unpaid debts mounting up behind her." Mrs Cooper tilted her head as she regarded me.

My shoulders drooped. It sounded like I wasn't the only person who fell for her bright smile and empty promises of payment.

"Oh, Grace, you too? I thought I taught you better than that." Her lips tightened into a thin line.

Now I had to shoulder the bad debt *and* Mrs Cooper's disappointment. "She always had such good intentions, and promised to settle her account once she landed the lead in the new show." Now I sounded like Agatha, full of enthusiasm for a future that would never happen.

Mrs Cooper *tsk*ed under her breath and shook her head. "We shall discuss that later, Grace, when you join me for tea on Sunday."

"Of course, Mrs Cooper." Once a fortnight I took afternoon tea with Mrs Cooper, and we dissected the latest fashion magazines from Europe and America. It was a lesson in training my eye to spot trends and how to apply them to outfits suitable for antipodean women. Apparently, our next appointment would start with a lecture on financial matters.

We said our goodbyes and left the church to hurry down the street to seek the shelter of taller buildings.

"I'm not sure that was your best idea, Grace," Sam murmured.

"Why?" I thought my response had been carefully worded.

She rolled her eyes. "Now everyone knows that not only were you the last person to see Agatha but that she owed you money."

Chapter Six

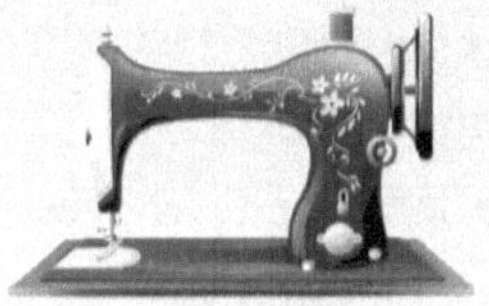

THE NEXT EVENING, THE SHARP RAP ON THE BACK door made me jump in my seat. Moments later, Frank pushed it open and strode in.

"Uncle Frank!" Theo hollered and hurtled at his uncle.

Frank ruffled the boy's hair. "What are you up to, small fry?"

"Poppa and me are making a boat." Theo held up a lump of wood and another block wrapped in sandpaper.

My men had moved on from housing projects for birds and were now constructing their own private navy. Which I suspect had been Dad's plan all along. They spent their evenings sanding the pieces of wood that would form the hull. Since Dad was a stickler for detail, the boat even possessed ribs, each no bigger than a finger. I only hoped the final result wasn't going to be too big to fit in any pond. Otherwise, we would have to sneak down to the Thorndon pool to sail it under a full moon.

"Frank. How's business?" Dad had more pieces scattered over the newspaper on the table.

"Good, thanks, Mr Sullivan." Frank kept his hat on, which deepened Dad's scowl that had appeared when Frank walked in uninvited.

"We won't be late, Dad. I have work in the morning." I fetched my bag and a light coat. Then I gave Theo a hug, which apparently I held too long as he squirmed away to rejoin his Poppa. A pang shot through my heart as I went out the back door. How quickly he's growing. If he reached the same heights as Frank and Freddie, I'd soon need to stand on a chair to see eye-to-eye with him.

Frank drove us towards Courtney Place and found a spot to park his vehicle. In a gallant mood, he rushed to my side to open the door for me, swept a bow, and then held out his hand as though I were some starlet emerging at an event. A smile flared inside me at the silly moment. He grinned as he tucked my hand in the crook of his elbow and led me along the bustling street.

"Dinner's nothing fancy, but thought you'd like to try this place." He stopped at a cafe with signage painted in green, red, and white.

Delicious aromas I normally only smelled wafting from Sam's place curled under my nose and made me close my eyes in delight. A slight pang of disloyalty to my Greek friend at being in an Italian cafe cut through me. But I would confess all when I saw her tomorrow and she would want to know every detail of the dishes I ate.

Frank held the door open. The interior was panelled with dark wood but had a rustic and cosy feel. Candles flickered atop red and white check tablecloths. Fat wine bottles in rattan sleeves hung from the corners. The overhead lights were dimmed by the thick amber glass of the shades. A mural painted on one wall depicted grapes being harvested by laughing women in flowing dresses.

Half the tables were occupied, and we sat beneath the mural in a corner at an intimate round table. We ate a simple meal of pasta with a tomato sauce and chunks of fresh fish, accompanied by bread dripping in butter, garlic, and herbs. Frank showed me how to suck up the spaghetti strands and I found myself giggling at the childish antic. I'd have to ask Sam if she knew how to make pasta, Theo would love a food he was allowed to play with. By mutual agreement, our conversations steered clear of Freddie, the war, or how Frank earned a crust. We talked of Theo and my plans to expand my business and offer a ready-to-wear collection.

"You're going places, Gracie. One day you'll be in the newspapers," he said.

My hand froze on my fork. Lord, I hoped not for the same reason as Agatha. Then the moment passed, and I shook it away. After dinner came dessert that Frank had insisted I try—a blush pink gelato.

"I need to see the owner, won't be long." Frank dropped his napkin to the table and rose.

The owner clasped his hands together as Frank approached, nodded his head and gestured to a door. The two men disappeared as conversation rose and fell. What business did Frank have with an Italian restaurant owner? As I pondered that question, I eventually decided I'd prefer not to know if the seafood had fallen off the back of a truck. Although it certainly tasted delicious and freshly caught. Perhaps Wellington had a seething black market for butter or tomatoes?

That made me snort, to imagine Frank overseeing an empire of ill-gotten vegetables and dairy products. Then the spectre of wartime rationing rose up in my thoughts, reminding me that hungry people could create a black market for virtually anything if it were in short enough supply. Last year a new spread came on the market called Marmite, and Theo and I loved to smear the black stuff over our toast. There were cries of disappointment when a jar ran empty. Although I couldn't imagine Marmite ever running out.

I refused to wait for Frank, which would let my ice cream melt and savoured each tangy, berry-flavoured mouthful. The last spoonful slid down my gullet as Frank returned to his seat. I arched an eyebrow as I licked the spoon clean.

"Business," he murmured. "But it's all settled now. How did you like your gelato?"

"It is the fanciest ice cream I have ever eaten. You may regret introducing me to it." I would bring Theo to the cafe one sunny weekend and order him a bowl.

"I'll bring you here anytime you want." Frank took my hand and tucked it into the crook of his elbow.

We left the cafe and strolled across the wide street to the Paramount picture theatre. They were showing *The Delicious Devil* starring Rudolph Valentino and Mae Murray. Sam and I had already seen it the previous weekend, but I could watch it over and over. The story was of a plucky heroine, working to support her family who, unknowingly, falls in love with a wealthy fellow. After many obstacles are thrown in their path, they finally have their happy ending. My seamstress heart loved the clothing and the glimpses of life and parties in New York.

Frank purchased our tickets, and we mingled in the foyer of the theatre. The push of people and wave of noise made me hold on to Frank a little tighter than normal. I prefer to watch crowds of people from a distance, rather than being in cramped quarters with them. Wellingtonians from all walks of life mingled as we clutched our tickets and popcorn, while we waited for the ushers to allow us into the cinema.

Frank called out to those he knew, spotting them in the crowd with his advantage of height. I enjoyed watching the women and making up stories about them based on their choice of clothing. Some of them still clung to the long and tubular shapes popular in the Edwardian era from before the war. A few dared a hemline edging north of their ankles and a slightly looser waist.

To further entertain myself, I made it a game to see

if I could spot a familiar garment that had started life in my shop. None were present this evening. Nor, in my opinion, was anyone dressed as fashionable as me. There was the advantage of my fortnightly teas with Mrs Cooper. My wardrobe had the latest European look months before it reached our shores.

"This way, Gracie." Frank tucked me closer and pushed through the crowd towards someone he knew.

Faces turned to me as we passed, and gossip sprang up in our wake.

"Are people staring at us?" I murmured to Frank. My skirt perhaps, with its cut and shape not seen much about on the streets. The soft green linen had a jagged handkerchief hem that swirled around my legs at mid-calf. I paired it with an armistice blouse. Mine was mostly a plain cream linen, with a geometric lace running either side of the square neck. And yet...there was a harsh edge to the whispers that prickled the hairs on the back of my neck.

"You're always a sight that catches the eye, Gracie." Frank winked and pulled me towards the bar.

Flattering as his comment was, I didn't think that was it. Then an oval face I recognised appeared, clinging to the arm of the man with a distinctive nose who had the nerve to peep into the ladies' lavatory.

"Miss Young," I said, hoping for a friendly reaction. Odd that she was out for a night of entertainment when Agatha had just been lain to rest the day before, or did she need the distraction?

"Mrs Devine." She halted and inclined her head.

"If you ever have some free time, I would love to see you at my shop to show you the designs I am working on. Miss Marshall always said you had a good eye for fashion, and I would appreciate your input." I put the offer to the other woman, wanting to do something to distract her from the pain she must feel at losing her best friend.

Interest flared in her eyes. "Oh, that would be lovely. Although I'm not sure if I have any time in my schedule."

My attention slid to the man at her side. Of average height, he possessed a stocky build that would be difficult to fit into an off-the-rack jacket. He seemed much older than Lynn, with lines carved into his face as though he found the world a constant disappointment or carried some worrisome burden on his shoulders.

"This is Mr John Marshall." The way she clung to his arm made me assume this was her soon-to-be-announced fiancé. I wondered if it was a coincidence that he shared the same surname as Agatha. She must have read my curious look, as she added, "Johnny is, or was, a cousin of Aggie."

"Mr Marshall, I am so sorry for your family's loss," I said.

"Are you indeed?" He stared at me for a long moment, then abruptly pulled Miss Young through the crowd.

"Rude bugger," Frank muttered under his breath. He watched the couple move towards the opening doors to the auditorium with a narrowed gaze.

"I suspect he is following the lead of his aunt. She had a bit to say to me after Agatha's funeral," I murmured. The memory still made me cringe at how she nearly accused me of murder in front of all those assembled.

Frank made a grunt in the back of his throat and his narrowed gaze followed the older man through the crowd.

"Do you know him?" I sheltered next to Frank as the crowd surged forwards when the doors opened.

"I know of him. He didn't serve. Family money kept him safe here, while we fought and died over there," he spat the words out.

A sense of indignation flared through me. Our brave lads gave their all and New Zealand suffered heavy losses in fighting alongside England and her commonwealth allies. Yet some used their privilege to keep their hides safe.

We found our seats as the feeling of unease continued to roll through me. Then pieces stitched themselves together in my mind. *His voice.* Mr Marshall was the man in the shadows of Agatha's memory. He had pointed his finger and told her to fix something. But what?

"What else do you know about John Marshall, apart from his aversion to putting himself in danger?" I whispered to Frank as the musicians played a quiet tune.

Frank glanced over his shoulder before answering. "Fancies himself as some big shot. He has plans to develop the waterfront, as though we are living on the Riviera, not Wellington. Apparently looking at the wharfs from his flash digs in Oriental Bay spoils his enjoyment of the harbour or some such rubbish. Wants to turn Queens Wharf into shops and flash apartments."

Personally, I liked sitting by the water but suspected I had salt in my veins like Dad. The shape of Wellington, somewhat like a half-closed hand, created a natural deep harbour. I always thought we were fortunate with how the city curled around the ocean. When I walked from my shop across Lambton Quay to the wharves, I struggled to think that once all of it had been underwater. A massive earthquake of less than seventy years ago had lifted the land and created the foreshore we see today. Perhaps one day, there might be a little plaque to mark where the water used to lap.

"But surely growth can only be good for Wellington?" I was grasping at straws to think a fancy redevelopment of the wharves had anything to do with Agatha's memory. The phrase *if I don't get what I want, then neither will you* kept bouncing around in my head. What had she done? Had she flashed her eyelashes at a councillor and ruined Johnny's plans?

Frank shrugged, then lifted his arm to rest on the back behind me. "That's not exactly the circle I move in, Gracie. But I can find out more if it's important to you?" A shrewd glint lit his gaze.

Was it important? Probably not, but it gnawed at me. "Please."

That easy smile flashed across his face, and his hand rested on my shoulder. "Anything for you."

Then the music rose in pitch as the red velvet curtains drew back, and I lost myself in the story unfolding on the big screen.

Summers lingered in New Zealand, even after the sun dipped below the horizon. The sky emitted a gentle light until well after nine. After the movie, we strolled along Courtney Place, music flowing from the open doors of bars and nightclubs.

"What do you say to a nightcap, Gracie? I can get you into the Cricket if you want." Mischief glinted in Frank's eyes.

I rarely drank, not wanting alcohol to make any silly decisions for me. Although I sorely wanted to see the place Agatha had thought would launch her film career, I had also promised Dad I wouldn't be late home tonight and there was work in the morning. "I would love to see inside the Cricket, but it's getting on to ten and I know Dad will be waiting up for me."

A scowl crossed Frank's face. "You're a grown woman. You don't have to keep some curfew like a youngster."

"Dad worries. Besides, I have work in the morning, and I have to get Theo off to Mrs Rogers. Not all of us keep gentleman's hours." I tapped his chest, teasing him out of the grumpy expression.

He caught my hand and held it to his chest. "I think I deserve a kiss then, in lieu of more time with you tonight. Then I will take you home."

Emotions warred in my gut. A note of unease that I had to offer some sort of payment for the drive home. A flutter of excitement to kiss him. A wariness that I was stepping off a wharf into deep water.

I raised my face to him, and he took the movement as agreement. Frank pushed the brim of his hat back and slid one hand to my nape. He kissed me slowly but with determination. The experience did nothing to settle the discordant thoughts running through me. Now, Frank had kissed me before. But they were light pecks on the cheek or a chaste brush of my lips. But apart from the day we waved them off to war when he snatched a parting kiss, this was the first time he had *really* kissed me.

"Now, that wasn't so bad, was it?" he murmured against my lips.

"You're not too bad. Almost as though you have a great deal of practice." I managed a shy smile while my mind whirled. Part of me had braced in case the intimate contact stirred up unwanted memories. But thankfully, my odd little gift had stayed quiet or mercifully dark.

Frank laughed and tucked me close to his side. A satisfied grin on his face as we walked back to the car.

Chapter Seven

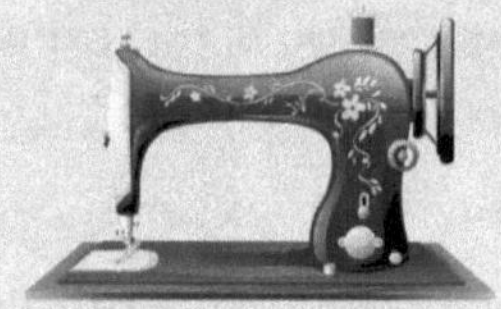

F RIDAY MORNING, THE BELL OVER THE DOOR RANG, and Joseph stood on the threshold. He glanced to where Etty sat at the sewing machine. A tiny suspicion nibbled at me that he was sweet on my assistant, but didn't have the courage to ask her out. His experience at war had roused within him a quiet sense of determination, but only to deal with those trying to kill him. It didn't extend to dealings with the opposite sex.

"Joseph, what are you doing here? Have you come to take us ladies out for lunch?" I called out from the cutting table.

Perhaps I could put the two together over a meal and see what happened. Rather like draping a piece of fabric over the dress form, and seeing if it wanted to be one thing or another. Setting Joseph and Etty side-by-side would give me an opportunity to observe if there were any signs of a potential romance between them. I had abandoned any romantic intentions for myself years ago, having been burned by that fire and still carrying the scars. But that didn't mean I couldn't give love a nudge for someone else.

My cousin removed his distinctive helmet and fidgeted with the chin strap. "I need you to come with me, Grace."

I set my pattern weights around a piece in the right spot on the silk and reached for the next one. "It will have to wait until after work, Joseph. Etty and I are rather busy today with the soiree at Government House coming up."

"It's business, Grace. Detective Archer sent me, and you are to accompany me to the police station." He spoke in a monotone, as though he read the words off a card.

Cold water gushed through my veins. "It's about Agatha." The words were dusty in my mouth. It was a silly thing to say. No other reason would summon me to the police station. It's not like they handed out invitations to afternoon tea.

He nodded. The sewing machine stopped, and Etty turned to scowl at Joseph. "You don't have to go with him, Mrs Devine. Not unless he's placing you under arrest for her murder."

God bless Etty and her revolutionary heart, who often complained that she had missed out on being a Suffragette like women in England or America. New Zealand had given women the vote the previous century, years before her parents had moved here from Ireland with a young Etty.

Pick your battles, Dad said and accompanying Joseph wasn't worth kicking up a fuss.

"I'm sure it's a simple matter that will be soon cleared up. You carry on, Etty, I doubt I will be long and we can go down to the wharf to eat our lunch afterwards." I fetched my hat and purse. Clutching the bag like a defensive weapon, I was ready to depart.

Joseph fell into step beside me, shortening his long stride. On Lambton Quay, horses and carts dodged around the trams rattling up the middle of the road. On the pavement, pedestrians diverted course to go around the tall constable. We walked to the police headquarters that occupied the corner of Johnston and Waring Taylor Streets. Newly completed in 1917, it was an imposing building made in the style of an old Roman palazzo. Concrete and rendered details had been painted to resemble Oamaru stone in some places, others were pressed red brick. If it were a dress, I would have called it overdone. As though the architect had thrown everything at it hoping to please everyone, but succeeded in pleasing only themselves.

There was little time to admire the interior details of the building, as Joseph led me through the bustling open spaces and along a corridor of what I hoped were offices and not cells. It reassured me they possessed wooden doors and opaque glass windows and not metal bars. He stopped at one and rapped sharply.

"Enter," a voice said.

I clutched my purse tighter in two hands, as though

I held a sword and shield and was unsure what to expect on the other side.

When Joseph pushed the door open, the detective rose from behind his desk. "Ah, Mrs Devine. Thank you, Constable."

I entered a spick-and-span office that would have passed a military inspection. On one corner of the desk sat a brass lamp with a green shade. The brass gleamed with no hint of a fingerprint which left me wondering how he turned it off and on. He dropped the paper in his hand to a neat pile in the centre of the green leather desk blotter. Everything on his desk appeared in perfect alignment with each other, and I imagined him using a ruler to perfect their placement.

His jacket hung from a hanger placed on a coat rack in the corner. The striped grey of his waistcoat was relieved by the ocean blue of his tie and the crisp white of his shirt. The fact he had removed his jacket improved my confidence a tiny amount. There couldn't possibly be any police brutality when he might risk a blood spot on his clean shirt. For some reason, my eye was drawn to the plain silver cufflinks holding his sleeves closed. Did he ever undo them and roll his sleeves up or loosen his tie?

"Do you want me to stay?" Joseph glanced between us and I wasn't sure whom he addressed the question to.

My heart pounded and while my cousin appeared to be suffering torn loyalties, there was still a comfort about his presence. "I'd prefer if Joseph stayed. Surely there is nothing to be said that he cannot hear?"

The detective gestured to a chair set against the wall and Joseph dropped to its hard seat.

"Why don't you sit here, Mrs Devine?" He pointed to the ladder-back chair with a brown leather padded seat on the other side of his desk.

With a glance at Joseph, I sat and rested my purse on my lap. "Am I to be interrogated, charged with murder, and dragged off to the cells, Detective?" I tried to inject a little lightness into the words to make the situation appear ludicrous, but my tongue stumbled over the syllables in my nervousness.

He stared at me, his dark gaze unreadable, and nothing softened the hard lines of his features. Not a single quirk of his lip, or the crinkling of his eyes in silent humour as he lowered himself back to his chair. "That remains to be seen. I want to go back over Miss Marshall's visit to your premises again."

"Of course," I murmured. It seems this interview would be all business with not a whisper of levity. The experience was rather like being called to the principal's office when you didn't know what supposed infraction had resulted in the summons. All you could grasp onto was a certainty in your own innocence, whatever anyone else might say. "What shall I do with Agatha's dress?"

"Her dress?" The detective repeated my words, one eyebrow raised a fraction. "Do you expect to reclaim it?"

"Oh, no, not the one she was wearing when…" my voice faded out as warring thoughts erupted in my head. Could I ask for it back? If I did, who would ever want to wear it again? Although the fabric might be repurposed, I suppose. "No, I meant the one she wore into my shop. When she changed into the gown, she left behind the day dress she had been wearing. She was supposed to collect it the next day. I didn't know if I am to return it to her parents or give it to you?" Glancing at his inscrutable face, I now felt it silly to bother him about an item of clothing.

"I shall inform the family. They can send someone to collect it from you." He selected a pen from the desk set and wrote a note on a sheet of paper on one side of his desk. "I wanted to go over your encounter with Miss Marshall since you were the last person to see her."

"*Second* to last. Surely whoever murdered her was the *last* person to see her." Indignation demanded I correct his mistake.

"Quite. Now, tell me about the fitting before the party." He picked up the topmost sheet of paper from the pile and his attention drifted downwards.

"She gave me very short notice, and I had to work all day on altering an older garment." I wasted my effort. How was I to know that Agatha hurried from me not to a party, but to a dance with death?

"But in our conversation, you failed to tell me she had been in your shop earlier that day." Detective Archer looked up and pinned me to my chair.

I swallowed, my mouth suddenly dry. "It didn't

seem relevant, since you asked me about her *last* visit, not her second to last one. Miss Marshall has been a customer for some two years. That day, she had dropped by in the morning to ask about a new dress for the party. That's why she returned later the same evening."

He didn't move, and his stillness prompted an attack of fidgets within me. I shuffled my feet and moved my purse on my lap. Glancing at Joseph didn't offer any relief from the situation nor any encouraging smile. With his head tilted back to the wall, my cousin stared at the ceiling with his eyes shut, as though he didn't want to bear witness to the interview.

"Why are you not telling me the truth, Mrs Devine?" The quiet tone held no anger, only disappointment. One black eyebrow arched as he posed his question.

That made a retort surge through me. "I am telling you the truth, Detective. How dare you imply I have lied. If you want, I can recite the process of cutting and altering a dress if you believe that learning about darts or lock stitches will aid in your investigation."

"I was referring to your rather public argument with Miss Marshall that morning." The eyebrow dropped back into place.

Oh. That. My hands tightened on the little blue bag as though it were a life buoy in a turbulent ocean. "When I told Miss Marshall it was impossible to complete a dress in such a short amount of time, she became somewhat insistent."

With deliberate slowness, the detective placed the sheet in his hand back on the pile and plucked another from beneath it. "We have a number of witnesses who were in Plimmer Steps that morning, and who came forwards about the argument they observed. One recollected some reference to money."

My heart stuttered and no matter how quickly I drew in a breath, I couldn't seem to catch any air. Was I too young to have a heart attack? Etty said it could happen to anyone at any time. Would I have time to dash off a note before I expired, to tell her she was right?

"It's all right, Grace. Detective Archer is trying to figure out who might have done this to Miss Marshall. She might have let slip something to you that is important to the investigation, even if you don't think it is," Joseph's familiar voice soothed a little of the panic racing through me.

The angry face of John Marshall swam before my eyes, yelling at Agatha to put something right, as she pleaded for more time. That seemed awfully relevant, but the stern-looking detective would at best dismiss me as mad, or worse, assume I was trying to conceal my own guilt.

"Miss Marshall can be rather forgetful about her outstanding accounts, but she assured me that she intended to settle her bill this week." She had promised double if she landed the role. Had any of his witnesses passed on that snippet or did they all paint me as some money-grasping murderess?

"How much did she owe you?" The detective jabbed at my sore point.

I failed to see how the tally of the debt was relevant. With a resolve I didn't feel, I met his piercing gaze and kept mum.

For the first time in our brief acquaintance, the detective had to fill the resulting silence. "You can tell me, or I can walk into your shop with a warrant and take your account books."

The monster. He wouldn't dare! What damage would it cause to my reputation if my clients knew their private dealings were laid bare at the police station? The amounts they spent on clothing as exposed and scrutinised as their bodies were in my fitting room.

The clasp on my handbag suddenly became fascinating, and I stared at it intently, while saying, "Nearly forty pounds."

The number didn't seem quite as horrible when I saw it in my ledger. Saying it out loud seemed like an admission that I couldn't run my business. Not helped by the sucked-in breath from Joseph. Dad would know by the time I got home tonight to compound the forthcoming lecture from Mrs Cooper. Although any rebuke was pointless now, the damage was already done.

Detective Archer rested his elbows on the desk and laced his fingers together over the stack of papers. "What an odd situation. Given the sum Miss Marshall already owed you, for some reason you still agreed to make her a dress at short notice."

He didn't phrase it as a question, which meant I didn't have to answer. But I would, just as soon as I figured out a plausible explanation. The goodness of my heart perhaps, or free publicity from having the socialite turned showgirl be photographed in one of my creations?

"What could she possibly have offered as an incentive?"

That was a question, and both my brain and dutiful nature compelled me to answer.

"Miss Marshall promised she would make good on her account after the party with an added bonus for my trouble." Even to my ears, it seemed a weak defence, and I simply couldn't tell him we had shaken pinkies on it.

My forthcoming trial played out in my head. A stout barrister with a curly horse-hair wig balanced on his head would rise to his feet, clutching the sides of his billowing black gown, and meet the stare of the judge dressed in an even more ridiculous outfit. Then my defender would clear his throat, before saying, *But your Honour, the deceased made a pinkie promise which is the highest degree of evidence of their intent to pay.*

Again, the single, doubting eyebrow arched. "Miss Marshall already had quite an outstanding account that she had failed to pay. Why would you extend her further credit?" Now the detective became chatty and questions positively flowed from him. "Or, perhaps, you were spurred into agreeing to provide a dress for some other, non-financial, reason?"

Damn Frank and his liquor-loosened tongue. When I dared to meet the detective's gaze, I found a hard glint reflected from his desk lamp. Good grief, he thought I did Agatha in!

I eased my tight grip on my purse before I put my thumb through the fabric. "Yes, she owed me money. So why on earth would I murder her before she had a chance to pay me?"

"Indeed," he murmured in agreement.

A single word from him, and the dread wormed deeper inside me. All I had done was point out that if I had some fatal grudge against Agatha, money might not have been my motive. Or that I might have another reason to want her silenced. The idea of the detective sniffing around my life conjured to mind a hunting dog that had the scent of its prey. They didn't stop until they had flushed out the pig and grabbed it by the throat.

After a few long moments, marked only by the tick of the clock on his desk, the detective called off his verbal dogs that were stealing the breath from my lungs. "Did Miss Marshall mention anything at all about her plans for that night? Such as whom she planned to see?"

My worried heart restarted. This was a question I could answer. "She stressed how important it was for her to land the role in the new show at the Cricket. She wanted to impress Mr Fleet—he's the owner of the venue. She didn't want another showgirl, Mintie I believe is her name, to get the part."

"How important was this show?" Bit by bit, he teased out the information from me.

"Very. Miss Marshall dreamed of going to America and starring in movies. Apparently, some big shot producer is holidaying in New Zealand, and Mr Fleet has convinced him to attend the opening night." Anyone could confirm that for the detective. Agatha spoke endlessly of how she would, one day, be a starlet.

He leaned back in his chair. "If you had to describe her mood that night, what would you call her?"

"Desperate," I whispered. Then I silently asked her forgiveness for saying it out loud. It seemed so impolite to call a dead woman desperate. But that was the only word I could apply to the wild look Agatha had in her eyes when she grabbed my arm and said I didn't understand her situation. Or when she threatened to reveal my secret if I didn't conjure up a dress.

Chapter Eight

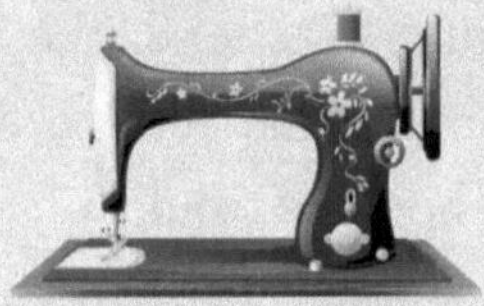

The detective released me, and I wandered back to the shop in a daze. Justice would prevail, surely? I most certainly had not murdered Agatha. So why did my heart stutter as though any minute Joseph might lay one hand on my shoulder and dangle handcuffs from his other hand?

My concentration for the afternoon was ruined, and when I tried to work, my stitches were misshapen. After unpicking a seam twice, I had to admit defeat. Instead, I took the account books and a stack of invoices to my desk in a screened-off corner and made sure every last penny was recorded. Both incoming and outgoing.

After work, I called out goodbye to Etty and found Frank lurking in the shadows once more. Concern crinkled at the corners of his eyes and made my bottom lip tremble in response. How easy it would be to throw myself into his arms and ask him to make the whole horrid affair go away. But I was never one for the easy route.

The poor fellow didn't get the chance to even say a word of greeting. There was too much indignation bottled up inside me. Like one of Dad's bottles of ginger beer that couldn't contain the pressure anymore, I was going to splatter the walls with frustration. Besides, I could always be frank with Frank and I needed to say my piece and relieve the internal burden.

"Can you believe Detective Archer thinks I did it? Me! How could anyone think I have anything to do with her death?" All afternoon rage had shaken up my insides. "How *dare* he imply I harmed Agatha!" I spat the words out in the quietest tone possible. People on the street had already told Detective Archer that I had argued with Agatha about money. No need to give them more rumours to pass on about how I flew into a temper tantrum.

Frank huffed a quiet laugh. "That just shows he's a useless detective. Anyone who knows you knows you'd never harm a fly."

We exited the lane and headed up Lambton Quay towards Thorndon. "Who do you think could have done it?"

Frank called himself an entrepreneur. Meaning he had plenty of cash to flash around, but no discernible job. I had an inkling of what he did to earn a crust. I wasn't oblivious to that side of life. Particularly with the *hoofers and molls* (as they were called in America) who wanted me to design them something special and it was paid for by their companions.

Besides, when my bare skin touched Frank's, I caught glimpses of a darkness in his life. Whether from the war, or whatever activities he did at home, I knew he walked in shadow. That was part of the reason I resisted his urges to make me, well, another Mrs Devine. I didn't want that sort of life for Theo. Easier to keep Frank at arm's length as my brother-in-law and uncle. Kissing him added a complication to that plan, and I'd not had the time to think it through.

He stared off up the road. "Lots of different rumours about who did it. Mintie, her rival for the part. Maybe a jealous boyfriend. Troubles at home. But I will tell you one thing for certain, Grace, no one thinks you picked up a spade and bashed her head in."

The pretend barrister in my head could add that argument to my defence. *Despite the evidence, your Honour, no one thinks the defendant did it.* I let out a slow sigh. "I wish more people would tell Detective Archer that. He thinks I followed Agatha that night with murder on my mind."

"Why would he think you had any grudge against her?" Frank came to a stop and turned me to face him.

I had kept the money issue to myself, certain it would resolve over time. "We argued that day. People in the lane tattled to the detective. He thinks I killed her in a rage."

"Argued about what?" Lines wrinkled his forehead as he stared at me.

"She owed me for a few commissions. But she had promised to pay me this week with a bonus for that gown if she landed the role." In my mind, pound notes scattered across the ocean and dissolved in the water.

"If things are tight, you should have said something. You know I'll always look after you and Theo. You're my family." Frank spoke in a measured, deliberate tone, even though his words were tinged with an odd mix of anger and frustration. I don't think I could ever recollect him yelling. At least not at me. But an undercurrent swirled around Frank like a dog straining at the lead. You didn't want to poke him too hard with a stick. If he ever lost his temper and it slipped his leash, you had better run and find cover.

Speaking of family reminded me of other things. Only now I had the bravery to confront him. "Why did you tell her, Frank?"

He tilted his head at me, a curious glint replacing the worried one. "Tell her what?"

I took his arm, mainly to get him moving again. Every time someone glanced our way, I wondered if they were listening in to report back to Detective Archer. As we turned into the next road, people dropped away. I had held my silence for over a week and it ate me up. Despite our public location, I had to let it all out.

"That day, Agatha sort of blackmailed me into making her a dress. She said you were drunk and confided in her, and told her something about me. She said she would tell everyone if I didn't find her a dress for the party," the words tumbled from my lips, finally free.

Only five people in the entire world knew my secret—me, Dad, Sam, Frank and Freddie. Now there were six, although two were dead, which left four. That still seemed like a big number, but mathematics had never been my strongest subject.

Frank swore quietly under his breath. "I never meant to breathe a word of it, Gracie. You know I'd never do anything to hurt you or Theo. I told you Agatha had a way of getting you to tell her more than you wanted, and then she'd use your secrets against you. I'd had too much to drink that night, and she seemed all sympathetic about how you married Freddie before we shipped out, when everyone knows I'm sweet on you."

Frank could brood and normally kept everything under tight control. But loose lips and a sympathetic ear had slipped under his defences. Had Agatha done something similar to the wrong person? Got close, learned a secret, and then dangled it to try to get something she wanted—like a part in a show? There was a motive for murder that might fit another and not just me.

I breathed out the last trace of resentment. Just as Frank knew I would never harm a fly, I knew it was extraordinary circumstances for him to slip up. "I know you didn't mean to, Frank. But I don't like that detective sniffing around my private business. What if she told anyone else?"

He grinned. "There's a simple answer, then. All you have to do is say *yes* to that question hanging between us, and you'll always have my protection."

If I married Frank it wouldn't be to protect myself, but Theo. Whatever arrows and rocks people threw at me, I would endure. But what stigma would attach to a nearly five-year-old boy and haunt him for the rest of his life? Theo idolised his dad and uncle as war heroes. Whatever my personal feelings about Freddie, I would never diminish his reputation in the eyes of his son.

"You know I'm not ready, Frank. Everything we've been through still rubs me raw, and I want to grow my business before thinking about getting hitched. If we put our heads together, I'm sure we can think of some way to nudge the detective off my trail."

"I can think of a way." The darkness crept into Frank's gaze, and I suppressed a shudder.

SATURDAY AFTERNOON, I sat on the grass of the Botanic Gardens and hugged my knees to my chest. Sam sat beside me and we cheered on Theo as he held the string to his kite, while Frank loped along to get it airborne. If a gust of Wellington's notoriously strong wind hit the paper kite, I feared it might take my child away with it and had asked Frank along to act as an anchor for the lighter boy, since Dad couldn't keep up with his grandson over rough ground.

"You need to stop worrying. Everything will work out once the police find the trail of who did it." Sam nudged me with her whole body, and I had to throw out my hands or topple over.

I chewed my bottom lip and despite my friend's advice...continued to worry. "What if they don't? I could end up in jail or hanged even! Then what would happen to Theo and Dad?" The two of them would probably muddle through as blokes do, but my heart would ache to miss seeing my son grow into a man.

Sam gently punched my shoulder. "Buck up. If the police are that dense, then we will have to figure out who did murder Agatha and hand them over. Then you can walk down the street with your head held high."

Privately, I thought Sam was mad if she thought a seamstress and a baker could do the police work of nabbing a murderer. But desperate people did desperate things, and I found myself entertaining her hare-brained scheme.

"Come on. What do we know about Agatha's last night?" Sam took my silence as permission to hurtle on down this mad road.

"I fitted her into the dress and she went off to the party. Except the police say she never made it inside and she was found next to the stables." Those few moments played over and over in my head. Agatha hurrying up Plimmer Steps towards Boulcott Street.

From there, Antrim House was clearly visible and only a few minutes walk.

"So there are two possibilities if no one saw her inside the house. One is that someone followed her and dragged her over to the stables. Or two, she planned to meet someone before heading into the party. Did you have any inkling of trouble in her life?" Sam clapped as Frank got the kite into the air, and Theo whooped in joy as it tugged at the string in his hand.

No need to ask what Sam meant by an *inkling*. Over the years, that word had become our code for—had any memories jumped from someone into my mind? "Yes. Her cousin, John Marshall, yelled at her to fix something. He said if he didn't get what he wanted, then neither would she. Agatha pleaded with him for a little time. I didn't recognise him at the funeral, because I had only heard his voice. It was on Thursday when I saw him again at the pictures that I realised why he seemed familiar."

"Do you think it was money problems? Mrs Cooper hinted she was racking up the bills. Follow the trail of debt and find whom she owed more money to than you and dump this problem at their doorstep." Sam poured lemonade into a glass and pressed it into my hand.

That was the other odd thing about Agatha. Her family was well off. There shouldn't have been any debts if they were paying her bills. Which meant either they weren't paying her bills, or she spent her allowance elsewhere. She certainly didn't spend it on fashion, since my account languished. But an argument over money didn't fit with the words flung by her cousin.

"I don't think it was money between them. Frank said Johnny is trying to get some big development started on the waterfront. What if Agatha did something to jeopardise that?" I gathered together the snippets Frank had told me. That Agatha liked to collect secrets and use them against people. Like me.

Sam snorted. "That would fit with what you saw. What if he meant if he didn't get his development, Agatha wouldn't get whatever she most wanted?"

"The lead role and her shot at Hollywood. But surely he'd never murder her over that? They were cousins." Family should stick together, not tear each other apart. Then old memories trickled through my mind. Every family has those capable of betrayal.

"Are you telling me you were never tempted to chase Joseph while wielding a shovel when you were younger?" Sam teased.

I picked a daisy and thought of those childhood summers on the farm. Nobody could annoy you quite like family. Joseph once grabbed an old rifle and waved it to stop me from following him. The next day I was chasing him away with a pair of hedge trimmers. "When we were kids, maybe, but never now we're adults. Something caused that fight between them and it was foremost in her mind that day." Over and over, I saw the way John Marshall peered down his nose at me at the movies. As though I had murdered his cousin. Or was he such a snob that he didn't like *my sort* who worked for a living?

The boys ran up and down the strip of grass as the wind buffeted the kite this way and that. My scorched heart ached. Frank doted on Theo. For now, though. One day, he would have his own family and less time for his nephew. Theo might not have a dad, but he had a granddad and an Uncle Joseph in his life to keep him on the right track.

"Let's put her cousin to one side for now and think of other suspects. What about another showgirl? That lot can be brutal off stage." Sam unwrapped the scones from the tea towel keeping them warm.

"Agatha mentioned Mintie as her main rival. She has the lead in the new show and has her shot to impress the Hollywood producer." Had a rivalry on stage spilled outside the Cricket? If there were only two contenders for the lead, how convenient if one were removed from consideration. I reached for the flask and poured a little cordial into a tumbler for Theo. The poor child was red in the face from the effort of both the kite and keeping up with Frank's long legs. Over time, his body would reach the same lanky build as his father and uncle.

He thrust the string at Frank and flopped on the grass like an exhausted puppy.

With a wink at me, Frank wound the string around a stick. "What are you two plotting?"

When it came to the world of showgirls, shady business deals, and thugs, I needed the help of Frank.

"I need to visit the Cricket, but during the day to talk to the girls there. Perhaps under the pretence of looking at their costumes or wanting a dance lesson. Is that something you could arrange, please?"

Frank nodded and took a fat scone with butter dripping off the sides. "Shouldn't be too hard. I can have a quiet word with Liam tonight."

That left the matter of her family and possibly a boyfriend, and I knew exactly who to tackle about that. Mrs Cooper. Then another idea popped into my mind, one so obvious I kicked myself for failing to see it. In every detective novel, they started at the crime scene. I needed to find where Agatha's life had ended.

"Frank, could you take Theo back to Dad?" I wouldn't normally ask. An odd tension simmered between Frank and Dad.

"Sure. Where are you ladies off to?" His hand stilled before taking another scone, a wariness in his eyes. No doubt his senses were alert to the whiff of a scheme in the air.

I gestured to the trees and what lay behind. "Sam and I need to go to Antrim House. I want to look at the grounds."

"You'll not find the Hannah family at home. They're at their farm up the Hutt Valley. Been there all month." He picked a sandwich and shoved it in his mouth.

"Who organised the party, then?" I tore another chunk off the scone to savour.

Frank swallowed and met my gaze. "Johnny

Marshall. Their family are old friends of the Hannahs and they were allowed to use the house. It was some charity fundraiser."

Well, that was interesting. What better way to ensure Agatha didn't get what she wanted than to control who got into the party she was desperate to attend?

Chapter Nine

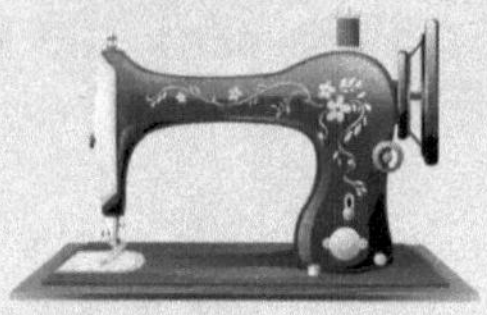

WE PARTED COMPANY FROM THE LADS, THEO RAN ahead of Frank who had the responsibility of carrying the kite with its trailing tail. Sam and I cut through the Botanic Gardens. A fantail flitted alongside us and at one point, darted back and forth across the path in front of us. I always thought my gift was like the little bird. You never knew when a fantail would appear, flit across your path, and then disappear again. They rarely lingered long, and neither did the flashes I saw from another's life.

The gardens turned into the old Bolton Cemetery, used by the first settlers to Wellington. Time weathered the moss-covered headstones to a peaceful area. The grass grew lush in the dappled light, and sweet peas rambled among grave markers, the flowers having escaped a bouquet long ago and gone wild. Roses and granny bonnets added to the sweet charm. The graves seemed less a reminder of the fleeting nature of life and more a quiet prompt to enjoy each day.

As we neared Bolton Street, the trees thinned out and lawn crept down to the street. Once on firmer ground, we set off along the road for a short distance to where Bolton Street turned into The Terrace. Arm in arm, we strode along in the sunshine until we spotted where Plimmer Steps rose out of the ground. Crossing the road, I stood by the top step and stared across at Antrim House.

Diagonally across from us and nestled in the ninety-degree turn of the road, was a white painted villa. A wisteria-draped porch providing a shady spot to sit in summer. Most of it was a single level, affording a good view of its grand neighbour.

"What do you think ran through her mind, as she paused here before darting across the road? Did she hurry to meet someone or was she followed?" A shudder ran over me as I thought of Agatha's final moments.

"If she was followed, wouldn't you have seen them lurking outside your shop when she left? It still wasn't that dark at eight." Sam tugged my arm, and we dodged behind a new motor to cross to the other corner.

"I don't recall seeing anyone. But they could have been up here on the street." Sam was right. If someone had loitered outside my shop they would have caught my eye as I waved goodbye to Agatha. Even Frank with his ability to cloak himself in shadow, wasn't entirely invisible when he waited for me.

We passed the villa and the grounds of Antrim House unfolded with its large trees and bright lawn. A smart black painted wrought-iron railing marched around the site. The sweeping driveway was flanked by three tall pillars. Two set far enough apart from the carriages and motorcars. The third pillar was only a small span away from its neighbour to create a pedestrian gateway. The drive curved back to pass before the stairs leading to the house, continuing on to the stables, garage, and outbuildings.

"Where do you think it was?" Sam murmured. She glanced around, but there were few pedestrians around on a Saturday afternoon.

There probably wouldn't be a sign proclaiming *here died Agatha*. We walked along a bit farther, trying for a better look at the buildings to the side of the main house. A pretty ornamental garden separated them, the roses in their hedged beds in full bloom. I recalled the article and the haunting photograph of the sheet-draped figure. The side of the building had a rose clambering up the side, and the detective had said she was found by the old stables.

"Under the banksia rose," I murmured, pointing to where the buff yellow rose clung to the wall.

We stared for a quiet moment, as though we expected a clue to rise from the ground. When nothing happened, another odd detail filtered into my mind.

"Agatha left behind the dress she had been wearing that day, and when I shook it out, an old newspaper article fell out." What had I done with the piece of paper? It must still be tucked into my apron pocket, hanging on its hook. "It was about a girl who died at school some ten years ago. Do you remember it?"

Sam shook her head. "No, but then neither of us went to private school. Why do you think she had it on her?"

I shrugged. "Maybe sentimental reasons, if the girl used to be a friend and she always kept it close? Or what if she intended to show the article to someone that night?"

Sam made a noise in the back of her throat, which sounded a lot like *I think you're barking up the wrong tree but you're my friend.* "Or there might have been an advert on the other side she wanted to remember, or someone else handed it to her, or it was a random piece of rubbish and she picked it up to toss into a bin when she saw one."

I sucked in my bottom lip. Sam was supposed to be helping me come up with ideas. "No. I can't shake the feeling there was more to that article. Why keep it for such a long time and then have it tucked inside your undergarments?" Given how it had shaken loose, I guessed Agatha had it hidden in her brassiere and pulling the dress over her head had tugged it free to tangle with the striped fabric.

Sam turned and leaned against the railing. She tugged on her fedora to shade her eyes from the unrelenting summer sun, but she at least appeared to be humouring me. "None of us know what she was doing that night."

"Frank said Agatha liked to pick at secrets. What if she discovered one about someone who struck back?" The showgirl had used a secret against me to get what she wanted. How many others had found themselves on the receiving end of Agatha's smiling blackmail attempts?

"If so, I'd say she learned her lesson about blackmail the hard way." Sam let go of the railing and wiped her hands together as though she had flour on them.

"I need to talk to her friend, Lynn Young. That day at the funeral, I brushed against her in the toilet and saw a flash of her saying *no, no, no, not again.* What if that memory meant Agatha had tried using a secret against someone? Maybe she had cautioned her in the past about doing it." The night I saw her at the movie theatre, I had invited her to drop into the shop to look at drawings. If I made it a more official invitation, would she accept? A fitting room worked somewhat like a confessional booth. Women opened up once their layers were peeled away.

"Come on, let's go home. If you cook dinner tonight, I promise to help prepare the vegetables." We linked arms and headed back along the road.

SUNDAY AFTERNOON I walked along Tinakori Road on a brilliant sunny day to Mrs Cooper's grand home. Under my arm, I carried a book of swatches. Even though it was the height of summer, I planned winter wardrobes. My mentor would cast her eye over the fabrics I intended to order.

Through the wrought-iron gates, I walked. I paused to touch the banksia rose with its creamy yellow flowers, another one of the last witnesses to what happened to Agatha. Mrs Cooper's gardener treated the plant mean and cut it back every winter to stop it from taking over.

Not being bold enough to rap on the front door, I went to the rear of the house. As luck had it, Mrs Cooper was already out on the brick terrace overlooking the garden. The surrounding trees were large enough to deflect the worst of the wind and only small puffs and eddies made it through their foliage.

"Well timed, Grace. I appreciate punctuality. There's something slovenly about people who are always late." She gestured for me to sit. A silver tea tray with porcelain plates in cream with a gold edge held a selection of crustless sandwiches and tiny cakes.

"How are you today, Mrs Cooper?" I sat in the white painted metal chair with the floral cushion.

"I am ageing like a vintage Bordeaux and only wish my Cooper had been here to witness it." A sad smile touched her lips.

The maid appeared carrying the teapot with steam puffing from its spout and sat it next to the matching cups, milk jug, and sugar bowl. Mrs Cooper poured and passed a cup to me. She waited until I was about to sip before beginning her lecture.

"How could you have let Miss Marshall's account go unpaid for so long, Grace? I always thought better of you."

While the mouthful of tea nearly choked me, I appreciated Mrs Cooper's direct approach. There was no beating around the bush, and you never had to guess where you stood.

I held the cup in two hands and tried not to slouch, which would trigger a lecture on posture. "She always had such a convenient and plausible excuse. Her allowance was being paid the next week. Or she just had to settle another invoice that was more pressing first. Or would I be a darling and wait until after the party."

Mrs Cooper let out a disappointed sigh. "Your heart is too kind, Grace. When will you learn?"

When indeed? My soft spot continued to leave me vulnerable to being preyed on by others. Freddie burned me in love, Agatha in business. "I can assure you, Mrs Cooper, that I always endeavour to learn from my mistakes and will not make the same one twice. From now on, if a client does not pay they will find my appointment book closed to them."

Thinking of the appointment book made worry churn inside my gut. Mrs Marshall's public accusation at the funeral and the whispers at the movie theatre haunted me. "I am worried though, at what impact Miss Marshall's death might have on my business. You saw the unfortunate encounter at the funeral with her mother. What if her words drive my clients to cancel their fittings?"

Mrs Cooper scoffed. "Then they are idiots. We have many fabulous events over summer and autumn, including the grand gala for the Prince of Wales's visit in April. No one will want to wear the same dress twice and we aren't exactly swimming in designers of your calibre in Wellington. Nor could they order something from overseas in time."

"I shall stay my course, then." And hope Mrs Cooper was right. Women had booked months in advance to ensure they had stunning gowns for when Prince Edward visited New Zealand. Agatha might have dreamed of Hollywood and being a starlet, but there were a number of ladies who wanted to try their luck at catching the eye of the bachelor prince and being whisked away to a fairy tale life in a castle.

"Good. Now, have you given any thought to expanding? The tenant above you is moving on and you can have the space at a discount if you have the courage to grasp it." Mrs Cooper sipped her tea and eyed me over the rim of the delicate cup.

My dream involved running my own fashion house. With the extra space, I could turn downstairs into a shop to display a ready-to-wear collection, and perhaps one fabulous couture gown to show women what was possible if they placed themselves entirely in my hands. Upstairs could be a bustling workroom with spacious private fitting rooms. There would even be room for my own office and a larger storeroom for all the fabrics I would need to have on hand. But such an expansion would mean hiring more than one more seamstress. I would need multiple staff, including girls to run the shop, even if I had the stock for them to sell.

"I wonder if it is too big a step. While I want to take on an extra seamstress, the idea of expanding over two floors seems rather daunting."

"Don't think of it as a daunting step. I view it as giving you room to grow. All mighty oaks started from a small acorn, Grace. Take the next step, trust in yourself, and I believe you will soon utilise every inch of both floors." She winked.

My heart swelled at her belief in me. Dad and Sam backed me, too. But to have the support of someone who understood the fashion industry made me want to stretch out my arms and fly.

"I am entirely motivated by self-interest, of course. You are developing into a designer as good as anyone in Europe, and I rather like being better dressed than those other old fuddy-duddies." She pushed the plate of treats towards me. There was always far too much, and I knew she would wrap something in a napkin for me to take home for Theo.

Laughter bubbled up in my chest. Some older women clung to the fashions from before the war as though time had frozen on November 1914. Mrs Cooper seemed unusual in that she embraced change and eagerly wanted to see what the new century brought.

I sipped my tea, feeling in a much better mood than

earlier in the day. "You will always be my favourite client, Mrs Cooper. I think even the showgirls don't lead the trends like you." The subject of showgirls brought to mind another topic that nibbled at my curiosity. "Do you know Miss Marshall's cousin, Mr John Marshall?"

"Johnny Marshall? Yes, he runs in our circle. Funny chap. He was born here but thinks he's more English than those of us who sailed over from Old Blighty. The fellow has never left New Zealand's soil, even during the war." She huffed a laugh and picked a tiny cucumber sandwich from the stand.

My mind struggled to see how her cousin could have been involved in Agatha's death, but I couldn't ignore the memory that surged inside me when she touched my skin. Or the convenient fact that he organised the party. "What does he do that is more English than you?"

Mrs Cooper leaned back in her chair and rested one arm along the rest. "He adheres to the class system. Doesn't like our kind mingling with the working class. The man is delusional. As if the nobility would have anything to do with *him*! Without wishing to cause insult, Grace, you are of working-class stock. He wouldn't approve of the friendship between us. Indeed, an afternoon tea such as we have now might not happen in England. You would walk a far steeper path there than you do here, Grace."

A chuckle escaped me. "I'm not sure about that,

Mrs Cooper. I've walked some pretty steep paths around Wellington."

"Ha! Quite true." She toasted me with her teacup.

Wellington was crisscrossed with roads that were not roads at all, but steep accessways to houses built clinging to the hills. One summer, Sam and I had walked up to Northland, the suburb sitting above Thorndon, by way of one such goat track called Military Track. It was so steep we had to stop halfway because I thought my calves were on fire and the only relief was to walk backwards.

"Why the sudden interest in the Marshall family?" That canny gaze studied my face.

I nibbled my bottom lip. It was one thing to seek fashion advice from the older woman, but I wasn't sure of her experience in matters of murder. "Since it appears I am a suspect in Miss Marshall's demise, I'd like to find a few more to scatter in the path of the detective. I wonder if there might have been some falling out between Agatha and her cousin."

Mrs Cooper scoffed. "More than likely, I would say. He never approved of her chosen career. Good, dutiful daughters are supposed to marry well, breed, and host charity lunches—not prance half-naked on stage. Leave it to me. I shall enquire if there was any bad blood between Agatha and Johnny."

Chapter Ten

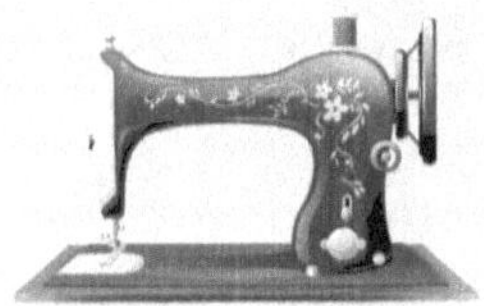

Monday, Frank telephoned to say Liam would introduce me to his girls and seamstress on Tuesday afternoon. The girls had Mondays off after a weekend of shows and Tuesdays they would begin rehearsing the new one. At midday, my stomach reminded me we hadn't stopped for a break, and I sent Etty up to the Kostas Bakery to grab something for our lunch.

As I swept the tiled floor of loose threads, the bell tinkled. Lynn Young stood in the doorway with a worried expression marring her face.

"Miss Young. How lovely to see you," I called out. She seemed in a grim mood to view my sketches, but perhaps she needed a distraction from her grief.

The other woman stepped inside and cast around her. "I have come for Aggie's dress. Her mother wishes to have it back."

"Of course. I shall only be a moment." Leaning the

broom against the wall, I entered the storeroom to find the paper-wrapped parcel. Glancing at my handwriting to ensure it was the correct one, I returned to find Lynn staring out the window at the passers-by.

She turned on hearing me approach and took the parcel, clutching it to her dress like a child with a stuffed toy.

Struggling for something to say to fill the eerie silence, I said, "Have you thought any more about seeing my sketches and a sample dress?"

A sigh heaved her shoulders and she shook her head. "Another time, perhaps. Now, I really must be on my way."

"Of course," I murmured.

She slipped out the door and down the lane towards Lambton Quay. Poor thing, she seemed in quite a state after losing her friend.

Later that afternoon, as the appointed time for my visit to the Cricket drew near, I packed a sketchbook and my pencils into a satchel.

"If I'm not back by five, could you shut up please, Etty?" I asked.

The busy seamstress had a pile of pattern pieces and assembled an outfit using the Singer sewing machine. Then the seams would be pressed open and the edges hand stitched down, to meet my exacting standards.

"Of course, Mrs Devine. I can't wait to hear all about it tomorrow." Etty waved me off, before returning her attention to the machine.

At the end of Lambton Quay, I turned right into Willis Street and marched along with purpose, keen not to keep anyone waiting. Frank loitered outside the red brick building that housed the Cricket. He lounged against his gleaming black motor with his arms crossed, watching the people hurrying by on the pavement. He pushed off the vehicle at the sight of me and tipped the brim of his hat back with a fingertip.

He stole a quick kiss and took my hand. "You sure you want to do this?"

My life had altered in less than two weeks, and I was determined to do something productive, rather than let worry consume me while I waited for the proverbial axe to fall. "If the police are nosing into my life, they're not finding who really killed Agatha. I can do my bit to discover whom it might have been and pass the information along to Joseph."

I had some sympathy for my cousin, torn between loyalty to family and the force. Whenever he saw me, his gaze shifted sideways and he shuffled his feet in such a way, that I wondered what the detective had whispered in his ear.

I stared at the facade of the Cricket, and excitement fluttered inside me. Most people swarmed along Courtney Place in the evening and went to the theatres to see a movie or a show. Tucked back from the main road, and along a narrower one, the Cricket performed revues in a style that combined burlesque and the Ziegfeld follies. Its patrons were those who preferred fast cars, fast women, and fast music. I threw fast cash into that mix too. Many a shady deal happened in the shadows of the club. Which was why my brother-in-law prowled its floor at night.

Frank pushed the door open, and we stood in a squat entrance that held the cloakroom and metal spiral stairs climbing upwards. A set of double doors with brass plates guarded the main room. With a wink, Frank pushed them open and held one side for me to pass.

I stepped into a different world, and my excitement dimmed. Devoid of external windows, the overhead lights were turned on for rehearsals and cleaning. That erased the magic that settled over the club after dark when only the small lamps on the tables and walls would emit a soft yellow glow.

A curving bar hugged one wall. Tiled with mirrors, it reflected the brightly coloured liquor bottles. Prohibition never had a chance in New Zealand. While it initially passed with a slim majority, by the time all the votes of our boys overseas were counted, it was soundly defeated. High walled booths covered in red velvet lined the other wall. The centre of the floor was dotted with round tables. Little ones were for intimate parties of two. A large one right in the middle of the room looked big enough to accommodate all of our extended family for Christmas dinner.

The stage was generous in size. Nowhere near the scale of the Grand Opera House, but sufficient for sashaying across while holding a feathered fan. The area in front was clear, providing space for the musicians to set up. Four girls were on the stage, laughing as they practiced a series of kicks and turns.

Mr Fleet hailed Frank and greeted us. An older gent, somewhere in his late forties with a solid appearance; he either shaved his head or had suffered complete baldness already. The way the light gleamed off his skull mesmerised me for a moment as I considered if he polished it.

He shook hands with Frank and then appraised me as though I were auditioning for a role. "Frank tells me you want to make outfits for my girls."

Nerves rattled through my body. I was a hopeless liar, so I stuck as close to the truth as possible. "Oh, no! I'd never be so bold, and I'm sure you have your own seamstress. I wanted the opportunity to study your girls and talk to them if possible. Young things are so bold with their fashion choices and ahead of what direction new collections will take. I hoped to use their style as inspiration for my clients."

Liam stared at me, and his eyes wrinkled with a narrowed gaze. "So you want to use my girls to line your own pockets?"

My mouth opened, but nothing came out. I glanced at Frank and then back to Liam. Was I supposed to pay for the privilege of sitting in the room while they rehearsed? Before I could reply, Frank stepped in.

"Don't tease her, Liam. You know darn well the girls would love to talk to Grace and maybe she'd be kind enough to sketch an outfit for your new show. You want Mintie to shine for this big shot producer, don't you?" There was a steel edge to Frank's calm tone and Liam straightened up, flashing me an apologetic smile.

"Sorry, Mrs Devine. I was only teasing, like Frank says. Do you think you could draw something for Mintie? Mrs Mac my seamstress is great, but she's better with a picture to follow and there's quite a bit riding on this show. We want it to be spectacular. There's a chance the American chap will adapt it into one of the new talkies." He gestured towards the stage.

Gosh. A talkie. I had read in a magazine that movies would soon allow actors to have a voice and speak to their adoring audiences. No wonder Agatha thought the show would be the career break she always wanted.

The gaggle of women onstage wore outfits that combined shorts, stockings, and high heels that would shock anyone on the street. Yet they were unconcerned about the amount of flesh they exposed. A cool blonde emerged from behind the curtain and with her arms outstretched, she glided across the front of the stage, making the occasional dip with her knees.

"The new show is a rollicking adventure with pirates. Mintie here is a princess whose ship is boarded on the way to her royal wedding. The roguish pirate captain takes her captive, but he is mesmerised by her beauty and dancing and they fall in love and she becomes his pirate queen. I want the girls in bright colours, so they look like expensive jewels."

"Pirates?" I breathed out the word. Gosh.

A swashbuckling romance played out in my head with men dangling from ropes as they locked swords. But I swept it to one side to concentrate on the matter at hand. Mintie with her ice blonde hair and willowy frame would look divine in cool tones. Excitement at the potential for the costumes bubbled up inside me.

"Pale teal and silver would be regal, with metallic embroidery to make her sparkle like sunlight on the ocean. It would also give her the appearance of a mermaid." My hand scrabbled in my satchel to find a pencil and pad as ideas burst in a swirl of colour in my mind.

"I never wear green," Mintie said in a cold tone, her pale blue gaze on me.

I met her stare. She might know how to wow men with her dancing, but I knew fabric and colour palettes. "I said teal, not green. The right hue will complement your eyes. Combine it with silver thread and perhaps mirror beads and you will resemble an ice princess."

The girls giggled and one snorted out loud. "That'd be about right. She can freeze you at a hundred paces that one."

"Ah, here's Mrs Mac." Liam gestured to an older woman carrying a tray with a teapot and an assortment of mismatched mugs.

She glanced in my direction and offered a shy smile as she set down the tray. Greying hair was tucked up under a pale yellow cloth and she wore an apron as though ready to do a spot of cleaning.

"Mrs Mac, this is Mrs Devine, a relation of Frank's. She has some grand ideas about costumes for the new show if you two could put your heads together." Liam waved in our direction.

Mrs Mac turned a curious gaze to me. "Oh? Am I being replaced because I'm too old?"

"No. Never," I reassured her. "Frank has indulged me by bringing me along to the Cricket. I'm terribly curious about the shows, but I've never seen one. I wanted an opportunity to watch the girls and offered to do some sketches, but you're under no obligation to use them." I didn't want to step on the other woman's toes.

She smiled, and it crinkled the corners of her warm eyes. "Let's have a seat and a cup of tea while we watch those young things prance around. I'm getting too old to stand all day long." Then she gestured to Liam. "Why don't you fellows go away and leave us women to talk all things sewing?"

I pulled out a chair at the table with the teapot and wondered at her exact age. She could be sixty, like Mrs Cooper. But Mrs Mac had the air of a worn woman whose appearance had been advanced beyond her body's years.

"Is your name really Mrs Mac?" Yes, the question was somewhat rude, but it seemed a curious name.

She snorted. "It's Mrs McIntyre, but this lot shortened it to Mrs Mac on my first day here."

That made more sense. "So it's a stage name, of sorts. How exciting. Have you worked for Mr Fleet for long?" I wondered what Mr McIntyre thought of his wife clothing showgirls. That led my thoughts down a rabbit hole of wondering what Dad would have to say about my visit.

Mrs Mac spoke as she poured strong gumboot tea into a mug and passed it to me. "Three years, now. Before the war ended, Liam got the old place ship-shape and back into business. Liam had served in the same unit as my son, and knew I needed work that wouldn't take me too far from home." She fell silent, staring into her mug.

Much was said in the silence. The war ruined so many lives and those of us left behind had to pick up the pieces and figure out how to carry on.

"What sort of fabrics do you normally work with?" I kept the conversation on safer ground than a mine-littered battlefield. Reaching into my satchel, I pulled out the sketch pad and opened it to a blank page. My pencils lined up beside it. I sipped my tea and sketched as the girls practiced their opening number. It helped to see how they moved and to imagine how fabric would flare out or swirl with each kick and spin.

Mrs Mac had a good eye, and over the course of two hours, we had the table top littered with sketches. She interspersed our chat with tales of what went on behind the scenes, and it only took a little prodding to elicit a few stories about Mintie and Agatha.

"I understand Agatha hoped to star in the new show. Did she and Mintie often compete for the lead?" I asked.

"Good lord, those girls fought like cat and dog. I

can't even think who started it now. Mintie once took in the seams on Agatha's dress and the poor thing was beside herself thinking she'd put on five pounds overnight." The older woman had produced a handful of coloured pencils and added shading to my designs.

Oh, dear, that was a mean trick to play. Not to mention more work for the seamstress to fix.

Mrs Mac picked up a deep blue pencil. "Then in retaliation, Agatha put a piece of broken glass in Mintie's shoe just before she went on stage. Cut her toes something horrid and she had to stay off it for a week."

That was a more horrifying tale, to actually cause physical harm to someone. The more I learned about Agatha, the more the darker side of her personality revealed itself.

"I used to wonder one of them didn't..." her voice trailed off. "Well, done is done now."

Wonder one of them didn't *end up dead*? I finished the sentence in my head.

She pushed the last biscuit towards me. "Since I have you here, perhaps you could help with something? Mintie wants me to mend her dress, but I'm not sure how to tackle a tear in organza."

"I'd be happy to offer my opinion." It would be something I could do to repay her kindness and time.

Mrs Mac rose and disappeared through a door to the side of the stage. She appeared a few minutes later with a beaded gown draped over her arms. Made of a black silk chemise with a taupe organza overlay, there was a tear in the left side above the heart. "She wore this to that party, says she snagged it on something on her way there."

"Mintie wore this the night Agatha...?" My voice dropped to a whisper, not wanting to mention the horrid event.

Mrs Mac nodded. Then she cast around, but no one was paying us any attention. "The other girls tell me Mintie was past fashionably late to the party and looked mighty dishevelled with a torn gown when she did appear."

Oh. Crumbs. My hands shook at the implication. Had a nasty rivalry behind the stage turned into a fatal one under a fallen rose?

"I can't see how to mend it without leaving a visible seam," Mrs Mac said, pulling my attention back to the fashion crime on the table.

"Such is the problem with anything see-through. What about turning it into a feature and embellishing it? A curving line of black and beige beads would match the rest of the gown and not look too out of place. A piece of nude fabric behind would add a little strength to the repair, but shouldn't be noticeable." I placed my hand under the tear and traced the jagged edge.

We discussed how to fix the gown, and I offered to take it with me as my thanks for Mrs Mac's time.

Then Frank unfolded his tall frame from a booth,

where he and Mr Fleet had been poring over what appeared to be account books. "If you're done, do you want a ride home, Gracie? This lot needs to get ready for opening time."

I glanced at my watch, the hands edging past five. Time ran faster when I was engrossed in sketching. I hadn't even noticed the girls fading away from the stage.

"Yes thanks, Frank. It was lovely to meet you Mrs Mac, and any time you want to discuss ideas you are more than welcome to call into my little shop. I'll have this repair done by the end of the week." I rested a hand on her forearm.

She gave me a tired smile. "I'd like to see your shop. Imagine me in a fancy atelier."

I folded the dress, then scooped my book and pencils into the satchel, and left Mrs Mac stacking the pages I had drawn. The topmost one, the shimmering design for Mintie to wear in the closing act.

Outside, Frank held the car door open for me. "Was it a worthwhile trip?"

"Yes. I discovered Mintie arrived late at the party with a torn dress." I gestured to the bundle in my arms.

Frank sucked in a breath. "Liam will be gutted to lose two leading ladies in as many weeks. But rather her than you. What will you do now?"

Haul out detective novels from Dad's stash in the garage and read what the plucky investigator normally did with a hot lead. Then a little voice coughed from

the back of my head. The detective must have interviewed those who attended the party and would
already know Mintie had been tardy.

So why did I still have the tickle at the back of my
neck, as though my every move was observed?

Chapter Eleven

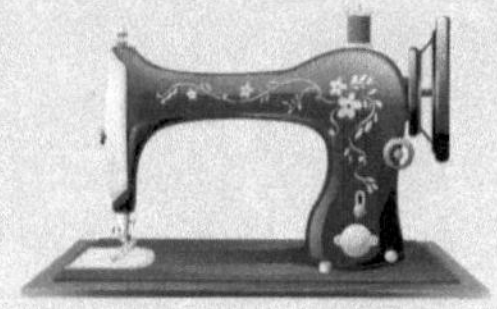

After dinner, Sam and I sat in the backyard on the old wooden deckchairs with a bottle of ginger beer each to enjoy the warm evening and to talk through events. Wax eyes flitted among the tall flaxes, sticking their heads into the dark red flowers to drink the nectar. I told my friend about my visit to the Cricket, and what I had learned about the animosity between Agatha and Mintie. In particular, how the latter arrived late to the party and the repair job I had taken away with me.

"So Mintie must have done it. The proof is the torn dress," Sam said.

"I wonder what happened." I recreated that night in my head and arranged for the warring showgirls to appear on stage at the same time. "Perhaps Mintie arrived by car, just as Agatha hurried across the lawn. They might have argued, drifting closer to the stables. Then there was a struggle which resulted in Mintie's dress being torn. Enraged, she grabbed a nearby shovel left leaning against the building and..." I didn't need to finish the sentence. Even in my mind, I blacked out the scene.

Sam huffed. "Sounds bloody obvious when you put it like that. Why hasn't that detective arrested her?"

"That's the bit that bothers me." I chewed over the same thing. The case against Mintie seemed much clearer than the hare-brained idea of me being involved. Yet the cool blonde had danced on stage and cast a critical eye over my drawings without giving away so much as a hint of being under the detective's suspicion. "He might not know about the torn dress. People he interviewed might have mentioned her being late, but would they notice a tear in the fabric? Especially if she did something to cover it, like wearing a shawl."

What if Detective Archer had examined Mintie as a suspect, and discarded her for some reason I couldn't discern? Or worse, barely glanced at the evidence against her since he had already made up his mind that I was responsible? "What if he still thinks I did it?"

Sam swung her feet to the ground and stared at me. "Have you spoken to Joseph and asked if they know about the dress?"

"No. I suspect he's avoiding me." And to be fair to my cousin, I only learned about the dress a few hours ago.

Sam screwed up her face at me in concern.

"This has been the first weekend he didn't come

around with his motorcycle to tinker on it with Dad and Theo." When I was young, I thought my tall cousin was a nuisance. As we got older, I realised the importance of family and it always warmed my heart how we had become closer. There was an easy rapport between Dad and his nephew and, one day, I hoped Theo would grow up to be the sort of man they were.

"Let's put Mintie off stage for a while and think about the other suspects. There's her cousin who seems likely, given the argument with him was playing on Agatha's mind that day. He organised the party and could have denied her entry if he wanted to retaliate against her."

Agatha's memory drifted through my mind. What did she and her cousin want that had depended on the outcome of the party? "Mrs Cooper is going to keep her ears open among her circle and find out if there was any bad blood between them. I keep coming back to what Frank said, that Agatha liked to collect secrets and find ways to use them against people."

I turned the problem this way and that. Then an idea struck me. What if Agatha collected a fatal secret that would help her cousin swing the vote for his development project? "What if Agatha was supposed to discover a secret they could use to ensure all the councillors voted for Mr Marshall's project? Frank said the party was some fancy fundraiser, those sorts of people might have been there. What would a wealthy councillor do to keep a sordid secret from ever being revealed?"

"You think whoever did it was someone who wanted to stop Agatha before she passed their secret on to her cousin? You would need to know who opposed the project." Sam twirled her empty bottle in the grass to make it stand upright.

"Mrs Cooper is my eyes and ears in that world. She will know." I liked that possible motive. Such a person would have far more to lose than a lowly seamstress. But it all seemed too uncertain and insubstantial. Like trying to make a gown from gossamer thin tulle.

Sam took the empty bottle from my loose fingers and placed it next to hers. I would return them to our kitchen to be washed and stored for Dad's next brewing session. "Moving on then. What about her friend, Lynn? She might know something, especially since she is engaged to Johnny Marshall."

I had been turning over ways to get close to the other woman. One way was to walk up and down the street outside her house, hoping to accidentally bump into her again. Although that might see me charged with being a nuisance as well as a murderer. "I have asked her to come to the shop to look at my sketches, but I'm going to make it into a free consult. If I can get her in a fitting room, she might let something slip. It might not work, but I don't have anything to lose."

"I'll pick at the lads who come through the bakery. They know all sorts of things and one of them might have a friend who is a domestic in the Young household. Which reminds me, what's this that you went out on a date with Frank and didn't tell me?" She cast a pointed look in my direction.

I wondered if all the men in Wellington stopped at Sam's bakery for their pie and a gossip. She always knew what was happening around town long before I did...wait, had it been a date? We had dinner, saw a movie, and he kissed me. My stomach flip-flopped. "I...I...thought we were just friends having a night out. It never occurred to me that he thought it was a date."

Sam picked up a pebble the size of a thumbnail and threw it at my head. I ducked, the tiny projectile skimming through my hair.

"Hey! What was that for?" I rubbed at my head, feigning hurt.

"Because I love you. And I want to stop you from making another idiotic decision." She took my hands in hers and shook them. "I don't trust Frank. What does he do for a living again?"

"He's a businessman," I muttered.

She arched one dark eyebrow. "Is he, now? Where would I find his place of business, then? Oh, that's right, down a darkened alley and operating from the back of a truck."

I hated it when Sam was right. If I could turn back the hands of time, I would never have fallen for Freddie's easy charm and been drawn into the world the brothers inhabit. But what was done was done. Besides, how could I ever regret Theo? "Our lives are intertwined because of Theo. What am I supposed to do, pretend Frank doesn't exist?"

Sam narrowed her gaze. That was clearly her preferred option. "Look, I'm not denying he's been a good uncle to Theo. But you don't want him as a husband and I think your dad has his doubts, too. There's always a frost in the air when those two are in the same room."

Personally, I thought Dad was as overprotective as Sam. Their hearts were in the right place, but I was a grown woman. "I'm not going to do anything stupid."

"Like kiss him and give him ideas he has a larger part in your life?" My friend's voice had a chill tone to it.

Well, okay. That was possibly a stupid decision. But it had been nice to kiss him, and I wasn't an old lady. A rare vein of frustration bubbled up inside me. "I'm not dead, Sam. Am I supposed to live the rest of my life like a nun, to make up for one stupid mistake from years ago?" It wasn't fair. Why were women punished for their missteps, but men got to carry on their merry way?

Sam slid off her deckchair and pushed me over to sit close. Her arm went around my shoulders. "Hey. Don't go getting all teary and snotty on me. Of course you can have romance in your life. You just need to be more careful about who with. I love you too much to see you get hurt again and you deserve better than Frank. Besides, if you want to talk about living as a nun, have you seen the desolate no-man's-land that is my love life?"

Laughter replaced the burn in my eyes. My bout of

self-pity was over as quickly as it had surged up. I threw my arms around Sam. "I love you. Maybe we should look for a respectable brother and sister who would suit both of us?"

She hugged me fiercely in return. "I like that idea. Could you ask Mrs Cooper to point us in the direction of a wealthy duo who goes skiing in winter? I quite fancy seeing what that is like."

We laughed and spent some time designing the perfect brother and sister who would sweep us away to a luxurious lifestyle.

"Oh, to sleep in past three and not have to get up and set the yeast to activate and then knead and proof long before the sun rises." Sam sighed at the luxury of a few extra hours in bed. "It'll all work out, Grace. You'll see. The dark years are behind us now."

I playfully tapped my friend on the shoulder. "Not your dark days, though. I don't know how you get up that early during winter."

The sun dropped behind the trees and the shadows crept across the lawn towards us. I picked up the bottles and hugged Sam with one arm. Wandering back to my house, I hoped that the dark years of war, disease, and misery were well and truly behind us.

FINDING some free time the next day, I set the torn dress on the cutting table and laid it out. Measuring the length and width of the tear, I selected a few of the beaded pieces to see which would suit the tear and not distract from the overall look of the garment.

Etty carried a basket of pieces over to the sewing machine and glanced at the sparkling gown. "What are you working on there?"

"It's a dress belonging to one of the showgirls. She tore the shoulder and I'm thinking of ways to repair it." I had narrowed my choices down to two different twisting vines that might work. One had a few leaves on either side, the other a single flower and lone leaf.

"The one with the leaves." Etty hitched her basket on one hip and tapped the more subtle piece. "The flower makes a statement but might detract from the dress."

"That was my thought, too. I think the dress needs to shine." Or, more likely, the wearer needed to command everyone's attention. Did Mintie ensure she would be the star to attract the attention of Hollywood by dealing with her rival with a shovel?

I pinned the vine with care, ensuring I caught the organza and silk underneath. Then I took the dress to the window and my favourite chair in the natural light. Once done, I had an excuse to return to the Cricket and seek out both Mrs Mac and Mintie. The brief lull this morning was only temporary. Day by day, our workload increased.

The visit by the Prince of Wales wasn't until April, but the society women needed a number of outfits for each event they would attend over the few days he was in Wellington. The brief stay would be topped off by a grand ball and most women wanted to out-dazzle the others. The evening gowns would take us the most time, and some customers still hadn't approved my final designs.

That thought made me glance at the telephone that sat silently on the wall. Why had they not rung to schedule their appointments? From memory, I had three clients yet to decide on which dress we proceed with and move onto fabrics. If they left it too long, we would have difficulty finding time for them.

Working the tiny, near-invisible stitches took all my attention. Regardless of the fact I wouldn't be paid for the job, I still did my best. It took time and patience, but by lunchtime I had the dress repaired to my standards. I held it up by the shoulders. The vine appeared to be a natural part of the gown.

I soon had Mintie's dress folded and wrapped. Then, deciding there was no time like the present, I fetched my hat and gloves and tucked the parcel into a wicker basket with a handle. "I'm off to return the dress. Shouldn't be more than an hour," I called out to Etty.

My assistant waved and returned to her work. The sewing machine purring away as I slipped out the door.

I set a brisk pace along the streets before my courage deserted me. Pedestrians thinned as I turned into the next road and headed towards the Cricket. On reaching the club, I stood on the pavement and glanced at the sign. Should I walk in unannounced? Only now did I realise I didn't know the etiquette of visiting showgirls. Frank orchestrated my previous visit.

What would Frank do? Finding a shred of bravery inside myself, I took a breath and tried the front door. Unlocked. Passing the first barrier, I used my momentum to keep me barrelling through the entrance and the next set of doors. My enthusiasm caused them to slam behind me, and the people clustered around the stage turned to stare.

"Mrs Devine?" Mr Fleet called out, an unsure note in his voice.

"Hello, Mr Fleet. I'm ever so sorry to barge in on a rehearsal, but I fixed Mintie's gown and wanted to return it." I waved my basket in front of me as I approached.

Five showgirls were sitting on the stage, their stocking-clad legs dangling over the side. Liam perched before them on a high stool.

Mintie stood on the stairs in the middle, a sheet of paper in her hands. Her cool blue gaze settled on me. "Fixed it? The dress is hopelessly ruined, and it cost a fair sum."

I swallowed, doubts assailing me under her scrutiny. I set the basket on a nearby table and pulled out the parcel. Untying the string, the brown paper fell away as I shook loose the dress and held it up before her.

She walked down the stairs and approached me with a feline sway to her hips. Nearing, she huffed. "A vine?"

"It covers the tear and I believe complements the dress without detracting from it." I slipped one hand under the shoulder and let the fabric glide over my palm.

"It will do, I suppose. I could wear it somewhere... mundane." She reached for the dress, bunching up the delicate fabric in her hand. Then her knuckles grazed my bare arm as she took it from my grasp.

Before I could protest that she'd made it sound like I had ruined her gown and made it only fit for searching in rubbish bins...a memory flashed over my skin.

Heavy breathing. Blood pounding in my ears. A hand roughly grabs the shoulder of my dress. The soft tear of fabric masked by a gasp and cry. "I have to get to the party." No one would stop me from shining for the Hollywood producer.

Chapter Twelve

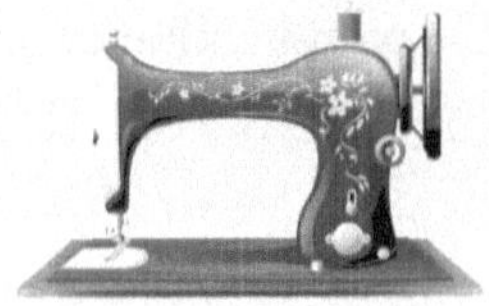

My brain took several long seconds to recover from the showgirl's memory.

"Mrs Devine? Is everything all right, you've gone right pale," Mr Fleet's voice pulled me away from the frantic moment playing in my head.

A deep breath shuddered through me, and I clasped one hand to my chest. "I'm so sorry, I think someone walked over my grave, and it startled me for a moment."

"Mintie has that effect on people," one of the girls called out.

The lead performer turned with a scowl and waved the dress at them. "Jealously is such an ugly colour on you Frances. When I'm a Hollywood star, I will have a wardrobe of expensive gowns much better than this old thing."

Her words cut through me. Despite what she had

done, Agatha had such stars in her eyes. "I think it's sad that Agatha never realised her dream," I murmured.

"Oh, please, that girl was never going to America." Mintie tossed the repaired gown over the back of a chair.

"We'll never know, now. She certainly intended to reach for the stars of Hollywood." All of a sudden, I felt a need to defend Agatha against her rival.

Mintie snorted and fixed me with a withering stare. "Agatha had a dream, that was all. I, on the other hand, have a plan." At my confused look, she continued. "I have my ticket booked on a ship that leaves three days after the show ends here. When I walk up the gang-plank, do you know what I will have in my bag?"

From her callous treatment, I'm guessing the gown I laboured over wouldn't make the cut. I shook my head.

A cunning grin spread over her beautiful face. "Letters of introduction and recommendation from Liam's producer friend. I already know which studios I will be approaching and my performance will ensure I have names as well. That is the difference between a dream and a plan. The only way Agatha would ever have made it to Hollywood would have been if Lynn booked her ticket and organised everything."

I only knew one Lynn in connection to Agatha, could there be another? "Lynn Young? Her best friend."

Mintie snorted. "Friend? Secretary more like. She used to trail behind Agatha and carry her handbag."

Mr Fleet coughed into his hand. "Thanks again for repairing the dress, Mrs Devine. Mrs Mac will be sorry to have missed you, but she's tucked up at home today." A worried look flashed over his face.

The thought of the older sewer added warmth to my smile. "Oh, I was hoping for a quick chat with her. I hope she is not unwell?"

Liam shook his head. "It's her lad, he...well, that's not my tale to tell. But he needed her more today than us."

Snatches of our previous conversation filtered into my shaken mind. Her son had been sent home from war with permanent injuries and Mrs Mac now had to care for him. "Please tell her to pop into my shop whenever she has some free time. I'd love a catch-up with her and to hear how the costumes for the show progress."

Taking my leave, I walked from the chilly club back into the sunshine. For a moment, I closed my eyes and let my skin drink up the heat. The last vestiges of Mintie's memories shook free. As I walked back to my premises, I turned over the brief flash that the dress had brought to the front of her mind.

Mintie had killed Agatha. There was no doubt in me now. It did not seem a cold, premeditated act, but more the result of an argument. A heat of the moment thing as their on-stage rivalry bubbled over with lethal consequences. It would surely only be a matter of time before the detective arrested her.

Then odd worries plagued me. Had I tampered with evidence by repairing the dress? By the time I pushed the door open to my shop, I was halfway convinced I would be charged for covering a tear so well that the damage was undetectable. Mintie should doubly thank me. Not only had I fixed an expensive item, but I had also erased evidence of her crime.

The afternoon passed quietly, Etty and I both intent on our different tasks. My three o'clock fitting cancelled, saying she had a terrible head cold. When I offered to pencil her in for next week, she declined, stating she wanted to fully recover before making another appointment.

"Odd," I murmured to myself as I picked up the eraser and removed her name from my afternoon schedule.

I returned to cutting out a blouse. Rounding the last piece, I set it on the pile and glanced at the clock. The minute hand swept towards the twelve, the hour hand about to land on four. My brain needed an early finish before I exploded.

The sewing machine fell silent as Etty finished her last seam and she snipped the thread.

"Let's finish for today, Etty, and start fresh in the morning." I gently carried the pile of silk pieces to my small storeroom.

"Oh, yes, please Mrs Devine." She pushed back her chair and carried the day dress to a bare form. Etty turned the garment to the right side and dropped it over the headless shape.

We tidied away the garments in progress and swept any loose threads or scraps from the floor. Then we parted company to head for our homes. Etty would take a tram to her flat in Wadestown, I decided to walk along the Terrace as I made my way to Thorndon.

Once home, I headed up to my attic bedroom and stripped out of my plain work clothes and shrugged into a loose summer dress. Before I found my friend to discuss murder, I needed to find my dad and son. Slightly below the level of our house (to accommodate the slant of the land) sat Dad's workshop. Voices came from the open door, and when I walked inside, I found dad working on a squat but rectangular piece of wood up on sawhorses. Theo helped sand, standing on an upturned empty beer crate.

"What on earth are you working on there? It looks like the side of a building." The smell of fresh pine and linseed brushed under my nose, and I drew a deep breath of what, to me, would always symbolise my dad and comfort.

"Project for a special client." Dad wiped his hand over the surface and then leaned down to peer across it, looking for bumps and imperfections.

With a fingertip, I followed a dark grain line. "It's gorgeous. This isn't pine though."

"Nope. Kauri. Dragged it out of a swamp on the farm some years ago. It's been quietly drying out, while I wait for it to tell me what it wanted to be."

"It wants to be the side of a building?" While he was occupied, I hugged Theo and kissed the top of his head. Obviously in a good mood, my son tolerated my affection and didn't shrink from my maternal touch.

Dad huffed. "This is the back of the piece. It will eventually be a cabinet and what a beauty she will be once finished and oiled."

In my head, I stood the item up and gave it shelves and drawers in the same rich timber. "Someone will be very lucky. We'll have fish and chips for a whole year when they pay you."

A smile tugged on the corners of Dad's lips. "Some things are worth more than money."

"Don't you start, or we'll never earn enough between the two of us to pay the bills."

Theo looked up, a frown on his brow. "Are we poor?"

Dad laid down his sanding block and ruffled his grandson's hair. "No, lad. We have each other and that makes us richer than many folk."

"I'm popping next door to talk to Sam. I'll be back in time to make dinner." I waved at the most important men in my life and headed out the door and across the lawn to find my best friend.

Peering in the window, I rapped on the glass with my knuckles before walking in the back door.

Sam sat with her feet up on the chair, a book open before her on the table.

"Mintie did it!" The words rushed over my lips, and I tried to lower my tone in case I alarmed Sam's mum.

"We talked about that with the torn dress." Sam looked up with one eyebrow arched, her attention divided between the book and me.

I pulled out a chair and dropped down, glancing at the open pages, wondering what absorbed her attention when my life and liberty were at stake. It seemed to be a cookbook, with sketches of the dishes in the middle of the page and frolicking vegetables around the edge.

"There's more," I said in an urgent whisper before I started reading the recipes.

"Mum's gone already to see Vita and the kids." She flicked the book shut and pushed it away. "What *more* have you discovered?"

Vita was Sam's older sister, and she had delivered four children in as many years. Mrs Kostas often helped with the brood, leaving Sam alone in the cottage. Which meant we had complete privacy.

"I mended the dress and took it back today. I did a pretty fine job, if I say so myself, and she wasn't even grateful." Whatever faults she had, at least Agatha was always enthusiastic and appreciative of my work. Mintie couldn't even rustle up a thank you.

"And?" Mild curiosity simmered in Sam's eyes, but I hadn't hooked her yet.

"When she took the dress from me, her hand skimmed my arm. And...that night...she did it!" I dropped my hand to the table with a thud on the last two words.

"You saw her kill Agatha?" Sam leaned forwards, eager for more details.

The flash of memory replayed in my head. "Well, not exactly. Blood was pounding in her ears. There was a struggle. The dress ripped. A woman cried out, and the only thought running through Mintie's head was that *no one* would stop her from getting to the party and being the star."

Sam let out a low whistle. "She argued with Agatha before either of them had a chance to go inside. You were right. They must have arrived at the same time."

I nodded and relief flowed through my limbs to my toes. We had the culprit and my life could return to normal. There wouldn't be any more stares or whispers behind my back. Or accusations at funerals. "Not only that, Mintie was so certain she would land the lead role that she has had her passage to America booked for some time."

Sam tapped the closed cookbook with one finger. "Why haven't the police arrested her then?"

I shrugged. "Perhaps they are waiting for more evidence or a confession?" From the little I had seen of the ice-cold showgirl, Detective Archer would be waiting a very long time for her to crack and admit to everything. That thought made a tiny strand of worry thread its way back through me.

THE NEXT MORNING I fell on the newspaper, fully expecting to see a headline announcing '*Showgirl arrested for murder!*' Instead the article announced '*Crucial clue found, could this crack the case?*' But annoyingly, they reported little detail about what the police had found. It had to be the torn dress, nothing else would bring the killer to justice. I tossed the paper to the tablecloth. Perhaps the detective was keeping it quiet about the discovery until he pounced. But my worries multiplied. With all the evidence against Mintie, why hadn't she been arrested? Had I missed some vital clue? I tried to clear my mind. I had pressing things to take care of, like a wriggly four-year-old and sketches waiting to be drafted into patterns.

Later that morning, I stood at the cutting table, sketches strewn about as I tried to decide which ones would appeal the most to my client. I couldn't sit, my body fidgeted, and I needed to be on my feet. Almost as though some horrible premonition nibbled at me, warning that a horrid series of events was about to unfold. Or not unfold, as I suppose it was more like a bolt of cloth that remained tightly wrapped and had yet to drop and unravel in a tangled mess.

I tapped my watch and glanced up at the clock on the wall. My ten a.m. was now a half hour late. "Etty, have you heard from Miss Drummond? Did she perhaps telephone when I wasn't here?"

Etty glanced up from her work and checked the clock. "No, Mrs Devine, not a peep from her."

How odd. But sometimes there was a clash of appointments, or a family issue might have arisen and she forgot to notify us. Unable to settle on a design, I gathered up the papers and returned them to a basket on my desk. I would re-evaluate them later, with a clearer head. To keep my hands occupied, I pulled out a piece that required beading work and took it to the chair in the window.

A little while later, the telephone rang. Etty rushed to answer it. That will be Miss Drummond, apologising for missing her appointment and asking to move it to another day.

"No, Mrs Smythe. Of course, Mrs Smythe. Very well then. Good day." Etty hung the receiver back on its hook and clasped her hands together.

"I'm assuming that was Mrs Smythe? We have her booked for a first fitting today at one." I glanced up, a seed bead balanced on the top of my needle.

"Not anymore. She has cancelled." Etty pulled out the eraser and removed the entry from the appointment book.

Two in one day? A cold lump settled in my gut. "No," the word rasped from my throat.

The next one came with the midday post. A brief note from another client cancelling her fitting the next day for a gown already cut out and pieced together. I balled the note up and crossed her name out with a red pen. Three clients who no longer wished to cross my threshold. The life and business I had worked so hard to create now seemed like a porcelain vase that someone had pushed off the mantel. I fell. All that remained was to shatter into a thousand pieces on the floor.

"Etty, why don't you take some hand sewing and go home? I don't know what to work on now, and need an afternoon off to think." Three clients with commissions in various stages that would now need to be carefully packed away and who knows if they would ever have their moment in the sun. To keep our hands busy, we could make more progress on the ready-to-wear dresses. If anyone would ever be brave enough to peer into the window.

We folded the gowns that were no longer needed with layers of tissue and placed them on a shelf in the storage room. Then I selected an outfit for Etty to take home that needed its seams pressed and felled. I refused to be defeated. We would continue, somehow. If my clients no longer wanted their fancy outfits for the prince's visit, then so be it. I had plenty of fabric, lace, and beads. We would use our time to make ready-to-wear garments. Among the bustling population of Wellington would be many a woman only too happy to snap up one of my designs.

My heart ached at the dark and rocky road ahead, but I had done it before and I could do it again. Just as our lads gripped their weapons and held their ground on a desolate battlefield, I was determined to survive. All I needed was a plan of attack.

I waved goodbye to Etty, her basket holding sufficient work to occupy her afternoon. Instead of heading home, I wandered down to the wharf, needing the whiff of salt and pound of the ocean to clear my thoughts. Maybe it was because Dad loved the sea. He had joined the navy as soon as he was old enough. Salt ran in my veins and part of my soul needed to have the water nearby to think.

I walked along the weathered timbers, thankful the heels of my Oxfords were too chunky to slip between the cracks. At the end were two benches, set a few feet back from the edge facing each other. Sometimes people came here to drop a line over the edge, and Dad brought Theo to catch sprats.

My limbs turned to stone as I glanced at the man with his attention fixed on the white peaks stirred up in the harbour.

Detective Archer.

The man whom my brain screamed was the architect of the slow destruction of my reputation and business.

He chewed on a sandwich, unruffled by the wind, the brim of his fedora resisting the gentle tugs from the breeze.

A gust of wind surged through me. How unfair that he appeared so serene while my life fell apart! I'm not sure what came over me, but I strode right up to him and planted my hands on my hips. "How dare you tell people I murdered Miss Marshall!"

Chapter Thirteen

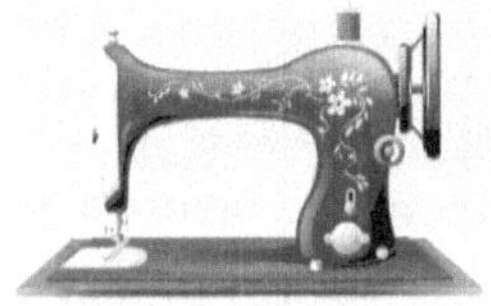

Detective Archer met my angry gaze with a calm one. He politely swallowed his mouthful before speaking. "I have made no such accusation against you, Mrs Devine."

"My clients are cancelling their appointments, afraid I will murder them in my fitting room. My business will fail. Is that what you wanted?" I had worked so hard, endured the harsh war years, and the terrible influenza that snuffed out lives in our homes. Finally, I was about to expand and spread my wings. I dreamed of a future where Theo lived a better life. Now it could all be snatched away.

Tears misted in my eyes, but the salt-laden breeze lifted them away as quickly as they formed. *No,* determination whispered from the back of my mind. Whatever happened, I would survive. Like the cheeky fantail who sheltered during the storm and came back when the sun came out, to flit among the trees. Once this horrid affair was over, and if I had to, I would pack up and start afresh in a new city, far away from the stigma that was attached to me here. As much as it would pain me to leave my friends, home, and the views of the harbour, I would do what was necessary to make a better life for Theo.

The detective put the remains of his sandwich down in the middle of the piece of brown paper in his lap and folded the sides over it neatly before tucking it into his coat pocket. Then he brushed his hands free of any trace of crumbs. "I am sorry that your business has been affected by the investigation, Mrs Devine, but again there is no such charge against you."

His words penetrated my brain. No accusation. No such charge. But those weren't the rumours circulating. Mrs Marshall was most adamant in her accusation at the funeral. "Mrs Marshall made a very public accusation at her daughter's funeral that I was the last person to see Agatha alive and they whisper I am your only suspect."

Gossip didn't have to be true to stick. Once breathed to life, rumours grew of their own accord.

He rose from the bench and walked to the railing, leaning his forearms on the cold metal. "You were the last person to see her alive. Or *second* to last as you informed me," he added before I could correct him, as I had done during my interview.

"What about the other showgirl, Mintie? Mrs Mac who makes the costumes at the Cricket said that she and Agatha were always at odds, playing nasty pranks on each other to sabotage their performances. Everyone said they were so competitive over the lead in the new show, they were surprised it hadn't spilled over into... well...something more serious. Then she arrived late to the party and in quite a state. Did you know about that?" My hands curled into fists. Yelling at the detective seemed as pointless as the waves battering the rocks. He remained unmoved by my plight.

"Of course. I have interviewed everyone in attendance at the party that evening, and those employed at the Cricket." Not a flicker of emotion passed behind his dark eyes.

Fear nibbled at me. Why couldn't he see that Mintie did it? She had motive and opportunity, isn't that what the detective always looks for in those pulp novels Dad loves to read? "Did you also know that her gown was torn?"

One eyebrow arched. Aha! Maybe he didn't know about that little fact. But I thought it might have been the *new clue* the paper reported that would solve the case. I tapped the left side of my chest. "Here. As though someone grabbed hold of the fabric during a struggle."

He turned towards me, his back to the ocean. Now a faint glimmer of interest sparked in his steady gaze. "And how did you come by this information?"

"I'm a seamstress. Mrs Mac asked if I could repair the damage. It's an expensive dress. There is no need to discard something because it is a bit battered. I was able to cover the tear with some beading and even if I have to say so myself, the split is unnoticeable." Inside my head, I pleaded with him to turn the full force of his piercing gaze on Mintie.

"So the dress was torn, but now is not?" He buttoned his jacket up as the surrounding wind became more insistent, tugging on loose edges of clothing.

My throat went dry. My worst fear confirmed. I had destroyed the evidence that Mintie engaged in a struggle that night. My tongue tried to return moisture to my lips, but the salt air dried them even faster. Think, Grace! Think! "You can see the repair work on the underside. If you look closely enough."

His groomed eyebrows remained impassive and gave no hint as to what knowledge sat inside his ruggedly handsome head.

I drew a deep breath. Crying would get me nowhere. Standing at the edge of the wharf, I stared out at the wheeling seagulls and wanted to scream at the implacable ocean, even though it would achieve nothing. "I've worked hard to provide for my son. Ask anyone who knows me, not a single person believes me capable of what some think I have done." I spoke to the choppy water, the ocean lifting the turmoil from inside me.

Detective Archer moved to stand beside me. His solid form was a most effective buffer from the wind. "I have interviewed numerous people. Yet the fact remains you were the last person to see Miss Marshall."

"*Second* to last. Mintie arrived late with a torn dress and looked dishevelled. Why is it so difficult to imagine that they both arrived at the same time, their animosity spilled over, and a fatal argument ensued?" I laid it out as simply as I could so that the truth would penetrate his dense brain. I pulled myself back from an edge, my throat eager to blurt out what I had seen in Mintie's memory when she touched the dress. But I couldn't. Not without looking deranged. The imaginary defence lawyer in my head couldn't stand up in court and say I experienced Mintie killing Agatha when our skin touched. Nor, technically did I *see* it happen.

"Miss Simmons has an alibi and is no longer considered a suspect." He tugged his sleeve up and glanced at his watch.

No! A gust whooshed through me and stole my breath. Impossible. Someone must have lied to protect her. But who? "What of the pivotal clue the newspaper mentioned? Surely that will implicate your killer?"

"I cannot discuss what was found. But I will uncover the truth, Mrs Devine, however inconvenient that might prove for the guilty party." He had a lightness in his tone that almost bordered on apologetic. But for me, or another?

Chaos erupted inside me on hearing he had considered Mintie and now had discarded her as a suspect. I would find out why, even if the detective remained tight-lipped on his reasons. I had to believe that my innocence would protect me. The police didn't imprison the innocent. Did they? I met his gaze with a tilt to my chin. "The truth will vindicate me. Then,

Detective Archer, I expect an apology from you for the damage you have done to my reputation and business."

He touched the brim of his fedora and turned, but not before I caught the smallest ghost of a smile on his lips.

I stayed by the water, taking the place on the bench previously inhabited by the detective. Sounds of activity drifted over me from the bustling wharves, where men unloaded ships and horse-drawn carts and trucks rumbled back and forth. I could see why Johnny Marshall wanted to develop the waterfront and make it more accessible for people. His plan would move the wharves farther along or up to Petone.

How easy it would be to curl up in a ball and cry that life wasn't fair, and I had nothing to do with Agatha's death. But we Sullivans were cut from tough fabric. Most likely sail canvas with such a tight weft a cannonball would bounce off it. Dad blew his foot off, mum walked out and left him with a toddler, and he still found a way to create a life for us both. No infuriating policeman would stop me from crafting the life I wanted for my family.

Resolve formed inside me and reinforced my spine. With it came a sense of calm. I would not be a victim in events. By taking a firm grip on the helm, I would weather this storm. Decision made, I nodded to the ocean for its companionship and then set a course for home. Or near to my home. Detective Archer might not have given me any insight, but a certain cousin would not avoid me any longer.

I collected Theo and we headed to Thorndon, my son skipping ahead of me and leaping over imaginary obstacles. My heart leapt into my throat every time he landed close to the road as a motorcar veered past, but he was apparently *too old* to take my hand for the walk. In our little cottage and tucked under the eave in my attic room, I stripped off my dress for a pair of wide-legged trousers and a simple blouse. With a plan forming in my head, I made a mug of coffee for Dad, piled some biscuits on a plate, and took them out to the workshop.

"You're home early, love," Dad said as he took the mug and toasted me with it. His salt and pepper hair was almost light blond from the amount of fine dust circulating after his labours on the large cabinet.

"My clients cancelled their appointments, and I sent Etty home with a basket of work." I wouldn't keep from Dad what was happening. We were too close not to share our worries. My hands needed an occupation, and I grabbed a broom to sweep up the sawdust and chips of wood.

His eyebrows shot up over the rim of his mug. "Trouble?"

My gaze darted to Theo, sitting on a stool next to his Poppa, munching on a biscuit.

"Nothing we can't weather. We just need to hold a steady course." Digging deep, I found a weak smile.

Dad nodded. "That's my girl. Don't forget to watch out for icebergs though."

I winced at the reference to hidden obstacles that

could sink a vessel. "Dad! That's such poor taste. You cannot make a joke out of such an event."

At the time, none of us could imagine a tragedy more horrific than the sinking of the *Titanic* and the loss of life in frigid waters. Then two years later, the Great War broke out and we drowned in horror.

"What's an iceberg?" Theo innocently asked.

"It's a piece of ice floating in the ocean and they can be bigger than our house. Poppa will tell you more about them. I'm going to watch out for when Joseph comes home, I need to have a chat with my cousin. Dinner might be a bit late though, depending on when he returns." I rested my hand on Dad's shoulder.

He reached up and squeezed my fingers. "Us men will survive, we've got a bit to do here."

I marched out of the workshop and took up position in the lounge, even though most of it was in shadow with the sun behind us. The armchair by the window afforded a view of the street and the house along from us where Joseph boarded. I didn't care how long it took, dinner was in the oven and no longer would Joseph avoid me.

A book sat unread in my lap as I waited. The clock chimed six before his motorcycle rumbled along the street, always thoughtful of his neighbours he drove slowly so as to reduce the noise the mechanical contraption made. That gave me time to hurry out the front door as he passed. With his attention on the road ahead and his destination, Joseph never saw me walking behind him.

Outside his home, he cut the motor and swung his leg over. Holding onto the handlebars, he pushed the Triumph along the narrow path between his home and the next. Then he wheeled the motorcycle around to the little shed where he stored the beast. Perfect. A quiet place for a chat and if I stood in the doorway, I would have him trapped like a possum. Hopefully, he wouldn't scratch to get out.

"Hello, Joseph." I leaned on the doorjamb as he fussed over the motorcycle and angled it ready to wheel back out in the morning.

"Grace." He glanced up, his eyes widened, and his Adam's apple bobbed up and down.

Good. He was nervous.

He inherited the Sullivan trait of needing to keep our hands busy while our brains ticked over. He grabbed a sheet to drape over his pride and joy, and it reminded me of how I tucked Theo into bed at night. Why did men get so attached to mechanical contraptions that made such loud noises and emitted petrol fumes?

I could have engaged in pointless chitchat, but we were family and I could cut straight to the issue with Joseph. Whether he liked it or not.

"I need to know why Detective Archer hasn't arrested Mintie Simmons." I crossed my arms and tried to appear intimidating. Not an easy feat with a six-foot-three-inch cousin and I only scraped in at five-foot-six.

His fingers tightened on the sheet. "I can't release details of our investigation…"

"Bollocks," I interrupted. "All I am asking is the reason *why*. She arrived at the party late, had a torn dress, and was dishevelled. Tell me why that doesn't add up to guilty. Help me to understand, Joseph, please."

He seemed to be holding his breath while he thought. Then he let it out in a sigh pushed between clenched teeth. "She has an alibi."

I arched one eyebrow and blew out a disbelieving snort. "Did she run to the party like Cinderella without a coach and trip in the gravel of the drive?"

He fidgeted with the positioning of the cover on the motorcycle. "She was with someone."

"Yes. Agatha. And a shovel." Mintie's memory flared through my mind.

Joseph shook his head, glanced at me, and then stared at the dusty toe of his boots. "She was with a man, Grace. A *married* man, which is why it's been kept quiet. He's some local bigwig and doesn't want his wife to find out. Dishonourable if you ask me, she should be told. But we're investigating a murder, not a cheating husband. Anyway, Detective Archer said what he told us was in confidence. Bloody stupid to do *that* in the back of a motor vehicle if you ask me."

"No, that's not right..." I started to protest. What would she be doing with a man? Maybe the two of them were involved in Agatha's murder? She might have learned the bigwig's secret and threatened to tell his wife. "Are you sure? He might be lying to protect them both."

He blew out a short sigh. "They were seen, Grace. One of the drivers parking a guest's vehicle saw them climb out of a fancy one with steamed up windows."

Slow realisation dribbled into my brain. The blood pounding in her ears. The gasp. The rough hand at her shoulder. A woman's cry. Oh, good gravy... she hadn't been bashing Agatha's head in with a shovel she had been...having intimate relations.

I slumped against the door and curled my hands into fists. I had been so sure. Frustration tingled along my arms. Why did I have this cursed ability if what it showed me was of no use whatsoever? "There was a piece in the newspaper, it said that a vital clue had been uncovered. What was it?"

His gaze roamed the shed, looking everywhere but at me.

"Please, Joseph. My business is suffering, and I need to know." Tears burned in my eyes but I blinked them back.

"A pair of scissors," he murmured. "Those funny ones shaped like a stork."

Scissors? Had the murderer tried to stab Agatha with embroidery scissors before resorting to the spade? Or perhaps they had fallen from a woman's handbag. Then a chill raised gooseflesh along my arms. I used stork scissors when I was doing fine work. A pair were tucked inside my sewing basket.

"Thank you, Joseph. I appreciate your honesty and you know I'll never whisper a word of what you told me to another." Except for Sam of course, because best friends had to know everything when a murder charge shadowed your life.

Joseph reached out and squeezed my shoulder. "Detective Archer is a good man, Grace. He'll find who did it, but he won't make his move until he has irrefutable evidence."

Chapter Fourteen

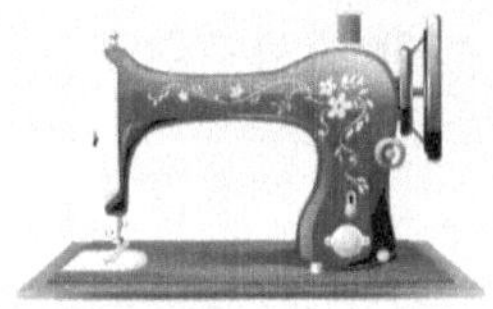

NATURALLY, I INTENDED TO TELL SAM everything. I had found my friend stretched out on the sofa in her lounge and scared a few years off her life by creeping up on her. Now I clutched a cup of tea and we huddled together.

Sam's brow wrinkled. "She was with a man? How could you not tell the difference in the memory?"

"I didn't see anything, just...felt...it." The excuse seemed weak even to me.

Sam burst into laughter. "Good God, Grace. It has been a long time if you can't tell the difference between sex and a spot of gardening."

I glared at my friend, this wasn't the support I needed. "I prefer to think that reflects badly on Freddie, not me. But I need your mind out of the gutter and back on murder. If Mintie didn't do it, then it has to have been Agatha's cousin, Johnny Marshall."

She tapped the side of her mug with one finger. "Did Mrs Cooper find out anything for you?"

"I've not heard yet, but she is in Monday for a fitting. Hopefully, she might have heard something about his proposed development." I spun through my memories for the earliest one caught from Agatha. *If I don't get what I want, then neither will you.*

Sam sipped her drink. "I wonder if he planned to use Agatha to get what he wanted. Perhaps a pretty showgirl to influence a councillor."

"Or someone good at digging out secrets to find blackmail material." Something else pressed on my mind. "Joseph said they found a pair of stork scissors where Agatha was killed. Like the ones I use."

A snort made Sam's drink slosh in her hands. "You and how many other women? Even *I* have a pair around here somewhere and I'm as renowned for my sewing as you are for your baking."

That eased a little of the worried churn in my stomach. Sam was right. The little embroidery scissors sat in practically every woman's work basket, not just mine. Anyone could have dropped them. The clock on the mantel chimed seven. "I better go, Theo will need dinner and a bath."

AFTER A WEEKEND SPENT PUTTING ASIDE my worries, they returned as a larger flock Monday morning. What would the day bring, and should I forget my plans to expand? Should I take on more space and staff if my wealthy clients are steering clear? Or do I see if I could compete with the ready-to-wear garments offered by Kirkcaldie and Stains? Either course was a risk.

"What's up with you, love? You've been chewing the rim of your teacup for a solid ten minutes now, and I don't think you realise it's not toast." Dad reached over and tapped the porcelain painted with bright yellow roses.

I lowered the cup to its saucer. There were some things I couldn't burden Dad with, but other problems could be lightened if shared. "Mrs Cooper is due in this morning. What will I say if she asks if I have thought any more about taking over the lease of the floor above me?"

"Do it, Grace. We'll find a way to make it work until your sales grow." He rose from his seat and on his way to the bench with his plate, he dropped one large hand on my shoulder and squeezed.

"It's a big step, Dad, especially with clients cancelling their appointments." It would take every penny and pound to pay the rent on that much space, without knowing if I could ever design, sew, and sell enough to claw my way out of debt.

"I know it's a risk, but sometimes you have to step off the well-worn and safe path and take a step into the unknown. If some clients cancel, you'll find others on your new path. Remember, this death and investigation will blow over and be long forgotten by the time the prince arrives to smile and wave at us in April." He dropped the plug into the sink and ran the hot water.

"You just want to design all the new furniture and fittings I'll need." I cleared away my breakfast dishes and placed them beside the sink for Dad to wash.

He turned and waved the soap shaker at me. "Of course. How can I turn down an expensive commission like that? We'll be eating steak for months."

We laughed, I hugged Dad, and we talked of possible ideas for the new space. Succeed or fail, you'll never know until you try.

I dropped Theo off at the childminder and entered my shop in a good mood. I surveyed our appointment book for the day. There was Mrs Cooper at 10 a.m. My afternoon appointments were crossed out. I refused to let it upset me. Instead, Etty and I started work on a few designs I had for casual day dresses that might appeal to the pedestrian window shopping along Lambton Quay, if I could find a way to lure them up the lane.

The morning flew by in a blur of activity, and bang on the dot of ten, my favourite customer swept into the shop.

"Good morning, Mrs Cooper." Always punctual, I had ensured the small fitting room was ready for my mentor.

"Good morning, Grace, Etty." She nodded towards my assistant, quietly hand sewing in the comfy chair in the window.

Etty blushed to the roots of her hair, being somewhat in awe of the formidable Mrs Cooper. Then she offered a shy smile.

"Your dress and overcoat are ready for the final adjustments." I gestured towards the fitting room.

We worked in advance of the seasons. While it was January and the middle of summer, I put the finishing touches to Mrs Cooper's autumn wardrobe before we started work on what she required for winter. I had sewn an autumnal outfit that would ensure she stood out during the ANZAC Day memorial services at the end of April. We chose a subtle tweed for its warmth and added small hand-embroidered poppies in a deep red. The outfit was a subtle homage to our lads who died on muddy battlefields and the poppies that grew over their graves. The red flower, a symbol of remembrance. Lest we forget.

I didn't have room for two dress forms in the fitting room, so the dress stood on the headless replica of Mrs Cooper while the overcoat hung on a padded hanger. Once I had helped Mrs Cooper out of her current garments and she stood in her petticoat, I removed the tweed dress from its form and settled it over her body. I did up the zipper and hooks at the rear, which elicited muttering from Mrs Cooper.

"I'm not sure I like those metal teeth so close to my body, but admit it does make getting in and out of one's clothing much quicker." She turned back and forth to regard her reflection in the mirror that covered one wall. Then she took my hand to step up onto the circular platform, about the size of a footstool that took up most of the space in the middle of the room.

"Zippers are a useful thing, but I agree not as tidy as a good row of hooks or an invisible button placket." I knelt on the carpet to adjust the final length of the hem. Plucking pins from the cushion tied to my wrist and using the tape measure to double-check where my eye said to tuck.

The zipper had been invented during Mrs Cooper's lifetime and had gradually moved into use in clothing with the advent of the twentieth century. Sometimes I sat back, amazed at the stories Mrs Cooper told of the last century. It seemed like a fairy tale, as she told me of her debut into society when Queen Victoria sat on the throne. A young Mrs Cooper had been tight-laced into a corset, before dancing the night away in a palace where noblemen vied for her hand. I doubted that the successful suitor mentioned his plans to take his bride to the young and dreadfully uncivilised country at the bottom of the globe.

Once I had the hem pinned to both of our satisfaction, we moved on to the coat. Mrs Cooper declared herself enraptured with the overcoat with its unique shape, which was really a sort of daytime opera coat. The back draped to a sharp point at knee level, anchored by a tassel ending in a deep red knotted ball, to reveal the lower third of the skirt underneath. The small detail that made my heart sing was the work I put into ensuring that the scattering of poppies followed the curve of the overcoat. The alignment wasn't obvious until the two pieces were worn together.

I placed the coat over Mrs Cooper's shoulders and adjusted the fall. She turned to the mirror and as her gaze drifted downwards, let out a gasp. Her hand hovered over the flowers.

"Oh, Grace, how marvellous. In Flanders Fields the poppies blow," she murmured the first line of the poem by John McCree.

My heart sang at her approval. "I am glad you like it."

"It is, well, *divine* my dear Grace. You have outdone yourself." She turned back and forth, admiring the view in the mirror. The flowers were small and a blood red. The reference to poppies growing from a desolate battlefield was subtle, I wasn't making a costume. "I don't know why you didn't call your business Devine Designs. Your married name is a perfect fit for what you create."

I swallowed and busied myself ensuring the tassel hung perfectly. "I've been a Sullivan for too long, Mrs Cooper, and my marriage was far too short. Besides, it seemed a bit presumptuous to imply my work was touched by the divine."

There were no adjustments needed to the overcoat, and I began the careful process of removing the new items and returning them to the form and hanger. Then I helped my client back into her summer outfit.

"You have done it again, Grace. Do say you will take the upstairs space and expand. I want to see my fledgling leap from the nest and spread her wings." She turned her back to me as I did up the hooks on her blouse. An oddly old-fashioned garment for the fashion diva, harking to an era when a wealthy woman had a maid to dress her.

My fingers pressed the last pearl button through its hole. "I am seriously considering your proposition. But I am concerned about clients cancelling their appointments."

She huffed. "I am aware someone is circulating the ridiculous rumour that you are responsible. I give it no credence whatsoever and know you will be vindicated. Stay strong, Grace. Besides, I suspect it will take some time to alter upstairs, and everyone will have forgotten this nasty business by then."

Her belief in me made tears moisten my eyes. If Detective Archer arrested me, I would certainly be calling upon the grand dame for a character reference. Setting aside my growing fears, I found a wan smile. "Dad suggested expanding in small steps, so I didn't overreach. That would give him time to turn the space upstairs into exactly what I want."

"Excellent! I knew you would come around. We have only the finer details of the lease to sort out." She tapped my arm with a glint in her eye. I wondered if she always got her way in the end.

Emerging from the cramped fitting room, Mrs Cooper elegantly sank to the leather armchair, and I pulled over a ladder-back chair as we discussed possible ways to arrange the two floors. Mrs Cooper was as excited as me for larger fitting rooms with comfortable chairs and mirrors on two walls. The idea of an Aladdin's cave to hold bolts of marvellous fabrics made me grin like a child on Christmas Eve. There was also room for a dedicated office where I could sketch under one of the windows, or do the accounts.

Mrs Cooper leaned forward and lowered her tone. "I thought you would like to know that I had a most interesting supper last night with a few friends. As you can imagine, the fate of poor Agatha was much discussed."

"Oh?" That perked up my interest and my hand stilled over my drawing pad we had been using to sketch possible layouts upstairs. With Mintie no longer a suspect, I turned my attention to Mr Marshall.

She gave me a conspiratorial grin. "I steered the conversation towards Johnny and his development for the waterfront. As luck would have it, one of my friends is married to a councillor. Boring chap, who voted for prohibition. Can you imagine it? But Annie Palmer has always been a good sort. She said that there were two men whose votes stopped the necessary permits, one being her husband, Charles Palmer, and the other Matthew Fadden. Apparently, at first, Johnny tried to woo their votes and turned on the charm. Then he became insistent and rather angry."

I imagined what part Agatha was supposed to play in changing the councillors' minds. A churning in my gut said it had something to do with her ability to collect secrets. I doubted a man who voted for prohibition would be swayed by a beautiful showgirl sitting in his lap. Or perhaps he had indulged in the delights found at the Cricket and didn't want anyone to find out.

Joseph's words whispered through my mind. Mintie had been with a married man who was some local bigwig. What if the councillor Johnny Marshall needed to persuade had become distracted by the wrong showgirl?

"Only two weeks ago, there was a nasty confrontation on Annie's front step. Johnny turned up unannounced, demanding Charles support the project or he would be sorry." She leaned back in her chair with a satisfied *what do you make of that* look.

"What do you think he meant by that—he'd be sorry?" I had my theories, but I wanted to know what a woman far more experienced in worldly matters than I, thought of such a threat.

Mrs Cooper scoffed. "I doubt he meant physical harm. Johnny was far too cowardly to pick up a gun and fight. His parents bought him a safe spot behind a desk here in Wellington." She tapped a gloved finger against her chin. "He might have some ruffians doing his bidding, I suspect his threat meant he had learned something about the councillors they'd rather keep quiet."

"Blackmail?" I whispered. It seemed the preferred pastime of the Marshall family.

"All of us carry secrets, Grace. Some flit close to the surface, others are buried deep. Some people don't want theirs exposed to the light of day and will do anything to ensure they stay hidden." Her voice trailed off to a murmur and her eyes lost focus.

I wondered if she contemplated her own secrets or those of her husband. Did it have something to do with why the wealthy noble couple packed up their lives in England and relocated to New Zealand? Gooseflesh erupted along my arms at the talk of exposing secrets and I rubbed the spots away with the heel of my palm.

"Is a building or some park really worth threatening people over?" There were other places Mr Marshall could develop around Wellington. If he built his fancy apartments up the hills, they would have commanding views across the harbour.

Mrs Cooper barked a short laugh. "Some men don't take hearing *no* very well, and they turn to threats to get their way. As it transpires, Mr Marshall has quite the temper when crossed."

Flashes of borrowed memory darted through my mind. I wondered how much of a temper Johnny Marshall had. Could he fly into such a rage that he would grab a shovel and smack his cousin over the head?

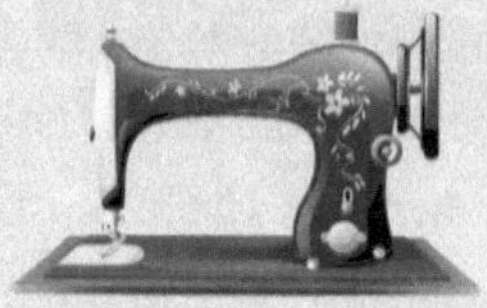

Chapter Fifteen

"I worry for his fiancée if he has such a violent temper." My hands smoothed the fabric but my mind thought of meek Lynn Young. Mintie said she trailed behind Agatha and perhaps she was of that particular type of personality that was accustomed to being moulded by others.

"Many women never truly know the man they have married until after the wedding. The woman he is courting in Auckland is in for an unpleasant surprise if she accepts him, I suspect." Mrs Cooper made notes on my sketch with a firm hand.

"But Miss Young is here, not in Auckland." No matter that we had known each other for some years now, I still had butterflies in my stomach when my mentor added her thoughts to a design, whether of a gown or a business layout, as in this case.

"Lynn Young? No, not that wee mouse, I am referring to the socialite Johnny has been chasing. He thinks we'll all be dazzled by a bride from up north." Here she snorted. "The deluded chap doesn't know being dazzled until he's seen the Crystal Palace fully lit at night for a grand ball." She let out a sigh and her features softened as she recalled the marvels of her youth.

Confusion flooded my brain, and my brows drew together. "But Mr Marshall is engaged to Miss Young."

Mrs Cooper handed the drawing back. "Is he? The cad will no doubt call it off now he's found something better. Such men often have a string of women who are only abandoned at the church door. While Miss Young is suitable for a meek little wife, I can't imagine her overseeing the table at one of our parties. Johnny wants a woman who can engage in *witty conversation*. Personally, I can't wait to take the measure of the newcomer when she gets here." A mischievous sparkle lit Mrs Cooper's gaze, and I suspected the new bride from Auckland would be taken down a peg or two if she thought herself superior to the Wellington set.

As my client stood to take her leave, I ran through events in my mind. Had I misheard, when Lynn complained Agatha had supplanted the news of her engagement in the newspapers? The sketch crumpled in my hands as my brain tried to snatch hold of the exact words. *My engagement to Johnny.* Poor woman. Had he told her that only she held his heart and they would announce their engagement once an appropriate period of mourning had passed? Or had her desire to wed, made an incorrect assumption about their relationship and she merely thought a proposal was imminent?

Try as I might, my brain couldn't recall seeing an engagement ring on her finger either in the church toilet or at the movie theatre when I encountered her. Not that the presence or absence of a shiny trinket proved anything about a man's whispered promises. Bitter experience had taught me that lesson.

With business concluded, Mrs Cooper waved goodbye with a promise to have her lawyer draft a new lease to cover the two floors that would soon be mine. Then I turned my attention to her hem. Settling in the armchair for the fine work, I dragged my work basket close and selected a spool of thread of a hue that would blend invisibly with the fabric. My hand groped for the cool metal of my scissors but found nothing.

Putting aside the dress, I concentrated on the contents of my work basket, moving aside the top tray with thread, needles and pins and checking if they had fallen below. "Etty, have you moved my embroidery scissors?" I called out.

"There's a pair by the Singer, Mrs Devine." She waved with a pattern piece from where she assembled a dress on a form.

Scissors were tools of the trade for us and the little shop had many pairs, each with a specific purpose. Pinking shears to stop an edge from fraying. Exceptionally sharp tailoring shears for cutting fabric. Special dressmakers ones with a sharp tip for cutting notches. And small scissors for snipping threads.

The glint of gold came from beside the reliable sewing machine and I picked up the little pair where the beak of a stork shaped the blades. Its feet turned into circles. The shape a reminder of when midwives used them to clamp umbilical cords. Although those ones were blunt. This pair was new, and not the worn ones with the plaited thread attached from my basket. Odd. I must have left mine at home when working on beading at the weekend.

Finishing the hem of Mrs Cooper's dress didn't take too long. Although it did take longer than usual, as I stitched slowly to ensure every single pass of my needle created a stitch of the exact same size. They might have been invisible stitches, but Mrs Cooper would still cast a critical eye over them. Once done, both garments were folded into a large cardboard box with tissue paper. Her driver would collect the box the next day.

As I worked, I considered and discarded how to find out more about Johnny Marshall and his quick temper. There was one obvious avenue—I needed to talk to Lynn Young. Whether she was engaged to him or not, she was certainly close to him, and she had been Agatha's best friend. What better person to know what went on between the two cousins?

I had already invited her to pop into the shop when I encountered her at the picture theatre and again when she had called to collect Agatha's dress. With the passage of a little more time, she might appreciate the distraction of trying on a few gowns. Given my new found fortitude to make the best of things, I decided to send her an invitation to try on a few outfits in return for her feedback about my ideas.

Finding a sheet of stiff paper, I wrote out an invitation and popped it into an envelope. I flicked through the telephone book to find her address and added it to the front in a neat hand. She lived in Kelburn, not far from the Botanic Gardens and an easy walk down to Lambton Quay, especially with the cable car to ride part of the way.

Before I could change my mind, I hurried along to the post office and popped the note into the box. With any luck, it would make the afternoon delivery. The next person I needed to tackle was someone who, though far taller than me, never looked down on me. Frank.

I needed to know if he had learned anything about Johnny Marshall. My brother-in-law was a more diffi-cult man to track down. Almost as though he didn't want to be found. With no expectation of anyone answering, I resorted to telephoning his house in Mount Victoria. An older woman with a terrible hacking cough answered. I hoped it was his cleaning lady and I asked her to let Frank know Grace wanted to talk to him whenever he was free.

Somewhat like summoning a ghost, having mentioned his name, Frank materialised outside my shop that afternoon as I locked the door.

"Message received," he murmured as he offered his arm and I placed my hand in the crook. He snuck a quick kiss and the glint in his amber eyes was tempered by the concern wrinkled at the corners. "How are you managing?"

"Clients are cancelling their appointments. Mrs Cooper informs me someone is saying I murdered Agatha, and they are worried I will either strangle them with a tape measure or stab them to death with my scissors." I tried to make light of the situation, even as it pressed on my mind. The mention of scissors made my brain freeze. "Scissors," I whispered.

"What about them? Do you need me to hide a blood-stained pair?" He chuckled, but there was a serious tone underneath that left me with no doubt he would assist, no matter how dark the task I asked of him.

"There was a newspaper article the other day about a vital clue that might bring Agatha's murderer to justice. I heard it is a pair of scissors." My hand tightened on his arm and I had an urgent need to turn our house upside down to find my missing pair.

He huffed and patted my hand in a manner meant to reassure. "She was done in with a spade, not stabbed. Some reporter got it wrong."

Yes. That must be it. Even though Joseph reluctantly confirmed the finding, Sam pointed out that almost every woman owned a pair of embroidery scissors. I tried to shake off the shadow that lingered over my skin when I thought of Agatha's last day on this earth.

"How is business, can you make ends meet this

month?" He guided us around a young couple hurtling along the footpath, in a hurry to make it to some unknown destination.

I squeezed his arm and renewed my belief that the truth would vindicate me. "The situation is not dire yet. Once the murderer is caught and everyone sees I am innocent, things will go back to normal."

He paused and placed a finger under my chin, tipping my gaze to meet his. "Promise me, Gracie, that if things get tight, you'll come to me?"

That was a hard promise to make. The Sullivan independence baked into my very marrow, demanded I take care of myself. The cautious part of me warned against being too indebted to Frank. A smile rose up in me as I found a satisfactory answer. "If I am at risk of Mrs Cooper evicting me, I will come to you."

The grand dame would never turf me out, but I might owe her a few commissions in lieu of rent by the time everything was resolved. I turned the conversation to a subject that I hoped would hurry along the proof of my innocence. "Have you learned anything of interest about Johnny Marshall? Mrs Cooper tells me he has quite the temper."

He glanced sideways at me. "I've heard a few things. He's quick to anger all right but useless with his fists. A wet behind-the-ears kid could knock him off his feet. Cunning bugger though, he prefers to use his position and money to push others around. He's not above shooting a few pounds at some desperate ex-soldier to rough up anyone that crosses him."

"Would that include his cousin?" A horrible thought, but I had to ask the question. Had one returned soldier hidden in the shadows cast by the stables, and waited for Agatha to dash across the lawn?

Frank made a disapproving growl. "It's not right to do that to a woman. If one of us did it, he deserves to have his neck stretched. I'm keeping my ears open, but I've not heard any whispers that a returned serviceman was involved."

My feet slowed as we approached the corner that Kirks occupied. You could take the shop girl out of the department store, but not the department store out of the shop girl. How I loved to stare at their window displays and the exotic wares for sale inside. Gazing at the luxury goods, reminded me of other things money could buy. Or not. "Apparently, there are two councillors who stand in the way of Mr Marshall's wharf development. A Mr Palmer and Mr Fadden. What do you know about them?"

Checking both ways, I pulled Frank across the road, navigating a path between motorcars, horses, and the electric trams. Then I halted at the corner of Lambton Quay and Brandon Street to stare at the wide expanse of glass. The scene within was a summer picnic with a white and yellow check blanket. A large wicker basket sat open, next to it delicate glassware and porcelain plates that would never survive a Sullivan family trip to the beach. The mannequin wore a summer frock in a blue patterned cotton with an inserted lace edge. A pretty outfit, but rather safe and adhered a little too strictly to the current trend for my tastes.

Frank waited as I cast a critical eye over the mannequin family, then we resumed our walk. He let out a chuckle. "You know nearly as much as me. You're turning into quite the information gatherer, Gracie. You'd have made a grand spy during the war."

I'd heard tales of the brave women who carried out secret missions behind enemy lines. "I think I am far too ordinary to be a Mata Hari. Nor do I want to live such an exciting life when it ends in front of a French firing squad." I had seen pictures of the infamous spy with her sultry eyes and her costumes that were little more than pieces of draped jewellery. She had performed before royalty and starred in moving pictures. Then she took French and German officers as her lovers during the Great War until being captured. I decided it wasn't the subterfuge to advance the cause that bothered me, but that she played both sides. That didn't seem like a fair wicket, as Dad would say. "You know I'm a terrible liar, Frank. I would never have got involved in Agatha's death if Detective Archer hadn't made me part of it."

Frank huffed as he always did at the mention of the policeman's name. "There are rumours that Marshall has something against one of the two councillors, and if the next vote doesn't go his way, there's going to be a very interesting newspaper article."

Snatches of Mintie's memory tingled over my skin.

Would the headline be '*Uptight councillor unwinds with Cricket delight?*'

"Do you think the councillor silenced Agatha before she could pass the information on to her cousin?" For someone who delighted in collecting secrets, finding her rival engaged in an affair with a married man would have been an irresistible morsel for Agatha. Did the man who voted in favour of prohibition have no qualms about taking up a shovel to defend his reputation as a pillar of society?

"Doubtful. That lot is even less likely to do violence themselves than Johnny Marshall. I wonder if he was bluffing, or perhaps Agatha was supposed to come through with something and didn't. Family can push us to do things we might not ordinarily contemplate." He fell silent and when I glanced his way, Frank had his jaw clenched.

I kept turning over how Agatha liked to collect secrets and that one must have cost her life that night. But whose? Johnny, Mintie, or a councillor?

"There's one person who might know—Lynn Young. She was in between the two of them and must have heard something." All I needed was a quiet and confidential chat with the other woman, and I was sure everything would make sense. That made another conversation rise to the surface of my mind. Mintie said that Agatha treated Lynn like a secretary. I wondered if that meant the quiet friend was privy to all sorts of things the showgirl might have been keeping to herself.

Chapter Sixteen

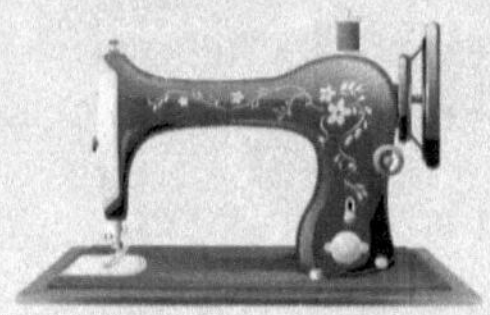

THE WEEK STARTED QUIETLY AND CONTINUED THAT way. No one crossed my threshold. My appointment book was scarred with lines like the rows of crosses marking the graves of fallen soldiers. I refused to be beaten and simply set aside the evening gowns and fancy outfits planned for the prince's visit and switched to making dresses and coats for winter. Whatever happened, I would have a small ready-to-wear collection of impeccable quality that I could offer to tempt pedestrian traffic.

Wednesday morning I sat down to breakfast and picked up the newspaper dad had discarded. In bold letters, it announced, '*Police stymied by clue unearthed by this reporter!*' The by-line then sought the assistance of readers in identifying the object unearthed by the intrepid newsman. It wasn't the headline that made my toast surge back up my throat, but the photograph. A pair of stork scissors. The gold plate worn from constant use. From one loop dangled a plaited length of embroidery silk to make them easier to find. Threaded through the end, a wooden S.

My scissors. The S stood for Sullivan and Theo had helped Dad make it for my birthday last year.

Heat flared over my limbs followed by a chill that made me shiver. "No," I rasped.

"What is it, love?" Dad looked up from the sports pages.

I held up the front page and tapped the photo. My throat dry, no amount of tea would relieve the ache. "These are mine."

He frowned. "What were your scissors doing where the body was found?"

An excellent question. And one for which I didn't have an answer. My panicked brain recalled my last interaction with Agatha. "I used them to snip an errant loose thread on her dress." The evening gown had no pockets, I had yet to figure out the perfect way to add them without ruining the line of an insubstantial dress. "She must have taken them for some reason."

But why?

Dad shrugged, and his lack of concern escalated mine. "Don't go borrowing worries, Grace. Maybe she grabbed them thinking to stab someone in the eye at the party." He winked and returned to scanning the results of the regional rugby tournament.

On the verge of scolding him for being so cavalier when my life was at stake, his words triggered my conversation with Mrs Mac. Agatha and Mintie were locked in an escalating feud. What if she took my scissors, thinking to use them to sabotage Mintie that night? Armed with the tiny weapon she could have snipped a hole in her rival's dress, or cut a shoulder strap. Or stabbed her in the eye while in the toilet, that would have ruined the other showgirl's career.

"Yes, that must be it." I latched onto Dad's explanation and used it as a life vest to re-float my belief that everything would be resolved soon.

Then a worry niggled at the base of my skull. Why hadn't Detective Archer asked me about them the day he interviewed me? Was he holding them back as his trump card, to be played when I was paraded up Lambton Quay in handcuffs?

My attempt to banish my worries didn't entirely work. Especially not when Etty arrived at the shop, her eyes wide with concern. "Oh, Mrs Devine, those are your scissors on the front page of the newspaper!" she blurted out before the door had even shut behind her.

"Yes. Agatha must have slipped them into her hand when she left that night." My words rang with a lack of confidence, but I had to cling to that sequence of events. Nothing else made sense.

"Why would she take your scissors?" Etty said as she stripped off her hat and gloves and hung her coat on a hook.

"I suspect she intended to do something to Mintie's dress, to ensure she didn't land the lead role in the show." If I said it often enough, I would convince my brain that was what happened.

"Gosh. What a horrid way to behave towards another woman." She tutted under her breath as she pulled the sheet from the form she worked on.

"I understand their rivalry had been rather nasty and, at times, violent." I sat at the cutting table with the latest fashion magazines spread out in front of me, taking my inspiration for winter designs.

"Still isn't right. If you are in a competition, then you need to work harder to be better, not pull the other person down." Etty stood with arms crossed before the dress form, as though she lectured it on sportsmanship behaviour.

"Quite right, Etty." Part of me had a tiny sympathetic pang for Agatha taking a pair of embroidery scissors to a fight where her opponent had a shovel.

After another day of companionable silence, I decided to close the shop at four that afternoon. With no clients to fuss over, we ploughed through more work than usual. I already had three completed outfits for my fledging line of pre-made clothing and another four cut out and being constructed. At home, I checked on Dad and Theo out in the workshop. My son sat at the bench with a colouring book and was intent on a scene with a soldier creeping through trees.

"Sam was looking for you," Dad said.

"Righto. I'll get changed and go find her." Up in my room, I stripped off my work clothes and changed into a light summer dress with a calf-skimming hemline. A heavier tread on the stairs heralded the arrival of Sam.

"Thought you would be home early again. Come

on, we're going out." She gestured for me to follow her back down the steep steps.

"I'm not in the mood, Sam. Those were my scissors on the front page of the newspaper." People stared and whispered before that article, now I would probably be pelted with rotten vegetables as I walked the street.

"You are not staying here to brood like a moody chicken. You're coming with me. Besides, we're not going far and there are some friends I want you to talk to." She grabbed my hand, and I had no option but to follow.

A groan escaped my throat. "I need to talk to you about Agatha. How can I do that in front of your friends?"

She grinned and, infuriatingly, refused to answer. Except with a cryptic, "Trust me."

Once out the front door, we linked arms and cut through the walkway from our street up to Tinakori Road and the Shephard's Arms. The pub had occupied the same spot since the previous century, when it used to be a coaching tavern for travellers to rest and change horses. I suspected it would still be there in another hundred years. It had a sense of permanence with its environment. Or perhaps it was its ability to adapt to events outside its cosy walls and meet the needs of its patrons.

The pub filled up with the late afternoon crowd of men out for a few quiet beers with their mates before it had to close at six. The practice had been instituted in 1917 to somehow improve the efficiency of our workforce. It was a daft idea if you ask me. All it did was promote the *six o'clock swill.* Men had a scant hour between knock-off time and closing time to down as much beer as they could. Politicians thought it would get men home to their families at a respectable hour, but many rolled in drunk as a result.

Sam waved to a man and a woman sitting in a corner surrounded by dark panelling at a small table. She made directly for them. "Grace, you remember Estelle and Harry. You two, be nice. I've known Grace forever, and I'd push you in front of a tram to save her."

I recognised the pair, being from what I thought of as Sam's *other life.* Just as I went off to the movies with Frank, Sam went to clubs with Estelle and Harry.

Estelle offered me a shy smile and a nod. Lacking in height, she had the Rubenesque figure once considered the perfect form and painters vied to immortalise such women in their work. With a dark cast to her skin and glossy black hair, I guessed she had Maori blood in her veins, but it wasn't polite to ask. The British took over New Zealand and treated the indigenous people appallingly. Then, in true British fashion, you weren't supposed to mention it and past crimes were swept under the rug. One day, I thought, things would change. Why did our boys fight and die, if not so *everyone* could be treated as true equals?

Of average height and a wiry build, Harry had a mischievous sparkle in his blue eyes and the most impeccably styled brown hair I had ever seen on a man. "Forever, huh? Then you need to sit next to me, Grace, and tell me all the embarrassing stories from her child-hood that Sam refuses to divulge. I rather think she has kept us apart deliberately, so we can't compare notes." He patted the chair next to him.

I shot Sam a look. My morose mood wasn't conducive to being social. I had hoped for a quiet chat so we could pull apart recent events, but then she had said to trust her. What was she up to?

"Did I ever tell you that Estelle here used to work in the Young household? She started as a maid but soon took over in the kitchen. She's head chef now at a restaurant in Courtney Place," Sam murmured.

Oh, I could have kissed her. My darling friend had found someone who would know more about the inside workings of Lynn and Agatha's friendship.

"Harry comes into the bakery to flirt with Ricky, my assistant. I'm not sure how successful he has been, but I admire his persistence." Sam waved to the bar manager and held up two fingers to order our usual. A shandy for me, a beer for Sam.

"Men can be a bit dense in the romantic depart-ment. Ask Sam to whack him with a rolling pin, that might make him come around," I said as I took my seat.

Harry laughed. "Oh, I think we have reached an understanding. I am worming my way into his confi-dence. I only hope I don't spoil my figure with the amount of baklava I am buying and consuming."

"You know you don't have to eat it all at once, Harry," Sam laughed.

I sympathised with Harry. Sam's baklava was a

sweet treat we adored in our family, but I didn't think I could eat it every day in an attempt to flirt with someone. Perhaps Ricky was being cautious with not openly displaying his affections. Sam and her friends walked a fraught path. Many Kiwis were uncomfortable with those who preferred the company of their own sex, and anything different to their own preferences was viewed with fear. And yet those same men failed to see the irony in how they clustered in tight groups at the pub and rugby clubs. It saddened me that people couldn't accept others for who they were on the inside. That Sam preferred to date women never affected our friendship. Just as she never judged me for my bad taste in men.

Well, she judged me a little bit. But it was done out of love.

"Did you work in the Young household for long?" I asked Estelle. Perhaps I might learn a few titbits about Lynn that would make her at ease, so she opened up, if I managed to entice her into my fitting room. Perhaps I should have offered baklava? That sparked another idea for my expansion...a plate of sweet treats for clients while they were being fitted.

Estelle looked to be a few years older than us and around thirty. She'd done well to climb from domestic work to the position as a restaurant chef. She sipped her drink before answering. "I was there for nearly ten years. I left a few years back as I wanted to be more than a cook in a private home. In some ways, the war opened up an opportunity. There weren't so many male chefs left for the few restaurants struggling on."

A moment of silence blanketed us, and we quietly sipped a toast to our fallen lads. "Were you able to keep your job when our boys returned?"

"Yes. I had made myself too indispensable to sack. But every day I have to prove my worth and deal with the criticism I should have stepped aside for a returned soldier." Her shoulders heaved, and she stared into her drink.

Women stepped up while so many men were overseas. We did their jobs and kept the country running. Then, after the war, we were supposed to all quietly slip back to our kitchens. But you couldn't give us a taste of such freedom and then rein us in. A change had been set in motion.

"What was it like in the Young household?" I pulled the conversation back to the topic much on my mind.

"I started off cleaning with my mum. I always wanted to cook and made myself useful in their kitchen until I found I was no longer cleaning and always had a knife in my hand," Estelle said.

"Were Agatha and Lynn always friends?" I smiled at Sam. I couldn't imagine a life without her by my side. Her parents bought the house next to ours when we were both infants. We went to primary school and high school together and always had each other's back.

Estelle shook her head. "No. Miss Young didn't have a lot of friends that I recollect. Certainly none that ever came to the house. Nor can I remember her having anything to do with Miss Marshall. Then, it seemed like overnight, they became the best of friends and were practically inseparable. Miss Young was always running around after Miss Marshall and dashing off to do things for her."

Shame Lynn hadn't embraced all secretarial duties and paid Agatha's bills. Then I might not be in such a pickle.

I wondered what brought on the sudden change to their close friendship. Girls did form into groups at school that often broke apart and reformed. "Do you recall when they became friends? Was it a recent development?"

"Oh, now you are stretching my memory." She winked and waved her empty glass at me.

I took the hint and excused myself to go to the bar and stand my round for everyone.

With a fresh drink in hand, Estelle took a long sip before answering. "They were at high school. Middle years, I think, as it was still a few years before I left. Let's see, that would make it about ten years ago."

Ten years. The number dinged in my brain. Why was that significant? Then I remembered—the old newspaper article. "There was a girl who died around then. I wonder if they both knew her and they consoled each other after her death?" That would make sense. Two girls bereft after such a tragedy might have supported one another and their shared grief turned into a tight friendship.

The barman rang his bell to herald the approach of closing time and the men in the room swarmed the bar to down as much beer as they could before walking home. We finished our drinks and said our goodbyes. We walked back at six, the sun still casting a light glow over the land. Summers stretched in New Zealand and often it was still light at nine. Terrible for getting a child off to sleep, but convenient for summer cricket matches in the park after dinner.

My mind was like a messy room with clues strewn everywhere. Now, I needed to pick them up and piece them together. "Thank you, Sam. There's something in what Estelle said that will help me figure this out. I just need to..."

"Figure it out?" She laughed and gave my shoulder a small push.

Chapter Seventeen

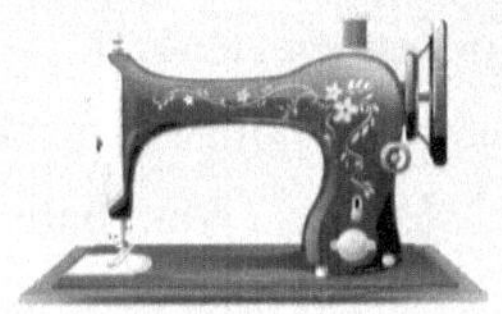

Over the next two days, I kept my eyes cast downwards and wore a hat with a wider brim for my walk to and from the shop. Heads turned as I passed and whispers followed in my wake. After the latest newspaper article, it seemed most of Wellington now knew they found my scissors beside Agatha's body. Everyone murmured why was I still at liberty? Even I questioned what Detective Archer was planning.

I imagined the policeman hiding behind every motor vehicle, tram, or door. Waiting to pounce upon me and announce, *you are under arrest!* Meanwhile, the gathered pedestrians would applaud his heroic actions in bringing the villain to justice.

The murder occupied my every waking moment, and I found myself wondering which bolt of silk looked more like blood. Snatches of conversations and glimpsed memories kept replaying in my mind. In particular, Mintie's words kept echoing in my head.

She had a plan, but Agatha only had a dream. Unless Lynn organised it for her. If Agatha was so reliant on Lynn, how did the showgirl expect to cope once in America? Although I had heard that Hollywood looked after their starlets. Her dream might have included a full staff to cater for her every need.

That made me grasp another piece of information. Mrs Cooper said Johnny Marshall was courting a socialite in Auckland. Did Lynn know?

As luck would have it, Frank appeared to escort me home. The scenario of my imminent capture now included a bout of fisticuffs between my brother-in-law and the detective while I was held captive by a group of women. I let out a snort at the scene I constructed. All it needed was a musical number.

"Everything all right, Gracie?" Frank asked with a glint in his eye.

"Yes, I think I need to stop watching so many pictures and need to read more books." On serious topics. Not overwrought romances with sheiks or pirates. I'm sure they would let me have books in prison. "You must know I am now the prime suspect in Agatha's death after my scissors were found by her. Although I am sure she took them from the fitting room that night for some reason."

"Knowing what Liam said about the fights between her and Mintie, I suspect she meant to plunge them into Mintie's back." He pulled me closer to his side and his shadow brushed over me. "I've been digging about Johnny Marshall for you, seeing what I can find. Ended up having a drink last night with a chap who drives for him. You were right, he's right miffed his cousin's dead. She was supposed to find what dirty little secrets those two councillors might be hiding."

I halted and gazed at him in surprise. "Oh. How did you manage to get that out of his driver?"

He tapped the side of his nose and winked. "A few beers and a couple of rounds of cards. Men like to grouse about their employers. They think they're better than us, but we see how dirty their bellies are."

"Do you think he killed her, because she didn't dig anything up?" I whispered, since people hurried home around us.

He arched an eyebrow and slightly inclined his head. Gosh. Family really could drive you to murder.

"How to prove it and get me off the detective's hook?" We reached the end of Lambton Quay and turned the corner and faced the incline up to Thorndon.

"I'll keep working on that. He's as slippery as a greased pig, that one. His driver said he went to the party early. But then he was hosting it, so he had to be there to ensure everything was set up right." He stopped at the usual spot where he parked his motorcar.

"Someone must have seen him slip out, surely?" If the detective had interviewed everyone at the party, someone must have said, oh yes, I saw Johnny Marshall lurking out by the stables with a shovel in his hands.

Frank placed a finger under my chin and tilted my face to his. Then he kissed me. When it turned a bit more serious, I gently pushed on his chest and broke away. Sam's warning rang in my head, and I knew I would have to talk to Frank. But not today. That reminded me of another relationship that seemed to be built on shaky ground. "Did his driver say anything about Mr Marshall and Miss Young?"

He shrugged one shoulder. "Not really. Says she's a quiet one. Does what she's told. Doesn't know about his trips to Auckland to see his other bit of fluff."

"Mrs Cooper said he's wooing the Auckland socialite and plans to marry her. Poor Miss Young. I wonder if she knows that there is another and that she will be set aside." I glanced at Frank and his jaw tightened. His brother had something in common with Mr Marshall, a way of toying with a woman's heart.

"Not all men play women, Grace. Some of us are loyal to the end." The glint in his eyes hardened, and I drew my hand back, not wanting to inadvertently touch any memory his words had summoned in his mind. Although I was a bit curious. Sadly for our boys, some women didn't wait for their man to return from war, and they switched their affections to one who stayed home. Had Frank kept a steady heart while some girl proved treacherous?

"I know, Frank, and I appreciate your loyalty to Theo and me. I was thinking about what Miss Young will do when the engagement is announced." We would both need a place to hide from society and lick our wounds.

"Maybe she'll go to America. It might be his parting

gift for her." He pulled the car door open and leaned on it.

"Why would Mr Marshall send her to America?" Agatha dreamed of being in the pictures. Perhaps her friend harboured a desire to write the scripts?

"His driver muttered something about how Johnny needed to pay for two tickets to America, but only if Agatha came through." He primed the motor, opening the clutch and doing a few half turns with the crank.

If I don't get what I want, then neither will you! The more I learned about the Marshall family, the less I liked them. He had dangled a dream before Agatha, in return for using her to dig up something he could use to blackmail the councillors.

"If I find out anything else, you'll be first to know." He gave a good half turn on the crank to start the Model T to life. Then he touched the brim of his hat and climbed into the vehicle. After making a U-turn, he headed back towards the main road.

Shaking my gaze away from the black Ford as it turned the corner, I carried on up the hill. Perhaps Lynn was better off free from Mr Marshall and Agatha. Out from under the Marshall shadow, she could live her own dream.

I SPENT a quiet Thursday evening at home. Theo and I sat together on the sofa as he sounded out words in a picture book. He was determined to be able to read when he started school and Dad beamed with pride from his armchair. Once I had Theo off to bed, I said goodnight to Dad and climbed the stairs to my room. After reading a few chapters of my book, I switched off the lamp and settled under the quilt.

Thoughts of murder, broken engagements, hidden secrets, and a duel performed by combatants armed with a shovel and a pair of embroidery scissors haunted my dreams. Eventually, I gave up. Angling the clock to catch the moonlight, it informed me it was four in the morning. Sleep evaded me. With thoughts swirling through me and nothing making sense, I did what always calmed the inner turmoil...I grabbed my sketch pad and a pencil.

Flicking on the reading lamp, I sat up and arranged the blankets around me. Then I laid the pad on my lap. In the middle of a blank page, I drew a quick sketch of Agatha, spinning before the mirror in the altered gown. Under her feet, in a fancy script, I inscribed *collector of secrets*. In another corner, I outlined the scowling face of her cousin, Johnny Marshall. Then I drew a line connecting them. Next to the line I wrote; *cousins, 'if I don't get what I want then neither shall you', short temper, councillors holding up the vote.*

While she had been discounted, I put *Mintie* in the other top corner and drew a beaded ensemble clacking against her knees. On the connecting line I added; *rivals, cruel pranks, vying for the lead, affair with prominent man.*

To give a complete picture, I had to do a quick self-portrait below Mintie and listed my money woes. Although it paled when compared to the possible motive of her cousin. To complete the square around Agatha, I drew *Lynn Young* in the bottom left. I connected her to Johnny with a line and wrote *engaged* with a large question mark. Between Lynn and Agatha, I wrote *best friends*.

A sigh heaved through me as I stared at the drawing. Something wasn't right. I needed to talk to Sam and at such an early hour, I knew where to find her. Dressing in trousers and grabbing a cardigan, I crept out of the house. I would be back before either Dad or Theo roused. Then I wheeled my bicycle from the shed and hopped on to zoom down the road and around the corner to the bakery.

A light shone in the rear of the bakery on The Terrace, and I leaned the bike against the wall and went in through the back door. Inside was warm, bright, and filled with the wonderful aroma of yeasty bread. Sam stood at a long wooden counter that Dad had built to be exactly waist height. My friend pounded dough before she shaped the loaves and dropped them into their tins to rise.

"You're up early." She flashed me a smile and carried on working.

"I couldn't sleep." My limbs were weary, which I suspected was fatigue. It couldn't have been the bike ride as it was mostly downhill. The return trip would take me longer.

"Jug is still hot if you want a cuppa." She gestured with her nose to the range and the bright red kettle perched on the rear element. "Then you can tell me what is interrupting your beauty sleep."

Finding a mug and dropping in a tea bag, I poured boiling water over it. Clutching the drink, I perched on a high stool at the end of the bench and out of Sam's way. "Something is bothering me about Agatha Marshall and Lynn Young."

"What's that?" Sam sliced off a section with a square blade and formed it into a rectangle before plopping it into the floured tin.

"From what Estelle said, the two weren't friends at school until that other student died. Then they were inseparable. Whenever I talk to Lynn, I am left with the impression she didn't like Agatha. Don't you think that is odd? You're my best friend and I love you, even if we don't always see eye to eye. Why would you be friends with someone you don't like?" I had dug out the old article and it crinkled in my pocket.

Sam made a sound in the back of her throat and then reached for a mug sitting on a shelf at shoulder height. She took a slurp of tea and considered my question. "If someone is a friend when they don't really want to be, then they must feel they have to. Like some obligation or their parents told them to play together."

"Obligation." I rolled the word around and considered what would obligate Lynn to Agatha. Feeling sorry for her, for losing her friend? But any such sympathy would have lessened with the passage of time. As the girls left school and made new friends in different social circles, their tie would have weakened. "That doesn't feel...strong enough."

She waved the swollen piece of dough that would keep rising once in its tin. "Then let's start at the beginning. Just like bread, you need the yeast to activate before you can do anything. We need to find the yeast that grew into murder."

I laughed at her metaphor, but I didn't have a better one to offer. "How do we find this murder yeast?"

"I'm going to ask you a question, and I don't want you to think about it. Just say the first thing that comes into your head." Sam dropped the dough into its tin and called out for Ricky. Her assistant took the tray away and would place the loaves by the ovens for their final rise.

"All right." It sounded silly, but I trusted her.

"Why did Agatha die?" Sam switched to rolling out buns and the small lumps were grouped together on a tray.

"Secrets," the word flew to my lips. Whoever held the spade that night, I was certain a secret was the reason. The only real question was how deep was that secret buried and could we unearth it?

"Do you still think her cousin did it because she didn't find any dirt against the councillors?" Another lump of dough was formed into shape and placed with its companions.

"No. He needed her ability to ferret out what people are hiding. It seems silly to kill the person you need. Rather like that detective thinking I did it because she owed me money. But once she's dead she can't pay a debt or dig up a secret. Nor can she use a ticket to America. But Lynn still could." As soon as I said those last four words, an odd sensation ran through me and gooseflesh erupted along my arms. Why was Lynn going to America when she thought she was engaged to Johnny?

"Who has a secret they would do anything to protect?"

Clutching the mug, I sipped tea and considered the question. Turning it around, who would do anything she was asked? Lynn—less friend and more secretary. But what secret could the meek woman possibly have?

"What if Agatha had a secret over Lynn, and that was why she ran around after her?"

Another soft plop and another bun was added to what became a tiny army of bread, waiting to rise up. "Estelle says she's been like that for years, always trailing Agatha and at her beck and call since that schoolgirl..."

"Died in the accident," I finished the sentence, but the word accident tasted odd on my lips. Bitter. False. A horrible thought leapt into my brain, and once my thoughts started down that path I couldn't haul them back. "What if it were no accident? What if Agatha killed her and Lynn helped her cover it up? That sort of thing would bind people together longer than sympathy or guilt."

Chapter Eighteen

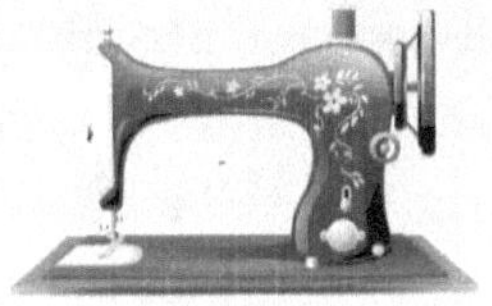

MY HAND DOVE INTO MY POCKET AND I PULLED out the old article. There was little detail, most of the piece detailed the young woman's few accomplishments and gave details of her funeral. Of Kate Burnell's actual death, it merely said she had been playing catch, had tripped trying to catch the ball, and dashed her head against a concrete step which resulted in the fatal accident. "There were only two witnesses to the tragedy, Miss Agatha Marshall and Miss Lynn Young. Both young women are being comforted by the families."

More details fell into place, and I jumped from the stool to pace the kitchen. "Agatha had an escalating rivalry with Mintie. Mrs Mac said it was only a matter of time before one of them was hurt. Lynn said Agatha always had to be the best at everything. What if she and this Kate were competing for something, and Agatha grew angry and pushed her?"

Sam blew out a low whistle and slapped her hands together to brush off excess flour. "Never cross a woman. But that still doesn't tell us who grabbed a shovel that night. Agatha hardly did herself in."

I had a horrible idea who might have. While I considered myself to have a calm disposition, there were rare occasions when I had snapped after life piled too much on my shoulders. Those were moments that galvanised me into action. Even the meekest and most downtrodden person could reach a point where they couldn't take any more. "Johnny's driver said he was buying two tickets to America. But what if Lynn didn't want to go? Agatha might have had this article on her that night to remind Lynn what she had covered up and to force her to keep playing the secretary."

"You might be right. Perhaps it was an accident after Lynn lashed out in frustration. You need to tell that detective and show him the article." Sam gestured at me with a rolling pin as she moved on to her next task, making pies for the hungry lads who would call at the bakery for their lunch.

"I will, but I want to talk to Joseph and see what he thinks first. He will know if Lynn was at the party that night and if they interviewed her." I downed the rest of the tea. Dawn was not far away as the sky lightened out the window. I'd better get home before Theo woke and found me gone.

"Until then, promise me you will stay away from meek but potentially murderous fake friends." Sam waved her rolling pin and pulled her dark brows together.

"I promise!" I hugged her, then pedalled home as the town stirred to life.

Friday passed uneventfully. Although a number of people slowed as they walked up the lane to peer in my window. Did they hope to spot a murder being committed within? By lunchtime I grew tired of the hands and noses pressed to the glass. With Etty's help, we moved the comfortable armchair out, and instead placed two dress forms wearing completed outfits. My first window display was nowhere near as good as those of Kirks, but we all had to start somewhere.

"We need hats and handbags to match, so they look like they are off to the pictures." Etty adjusted the hang of the dropped waist on a teal and black striped dress.

Handbags we could make ourselves. All that was required were frames, which I had in the storeroom, and scraps of fabric. "I'll find a couple of frames that we can cover and embellish for these two." Hats were trickier, and I had yet to establish a relationship with a milliner, to craft hats to go with my designs.

I made a mental list of things to do. Befriend a milliner went on there, along with buy more dress forms. I couldn't make and display gowns without them. As the afternoon lengthened, I sent Etty home to start her weekend early. My perfect employee took the pieces she needed to make a handbag. "It'll give me something to do Sunday afternoon."

I swept the floors and tidied up, stuffing the scraps of fabric into baskets and stowing them away in the storeroom. Then I turned my attention to the sewing machine. I would give it an oil and check the needle. The reliable Singer had worked hard all week. With that done, I decided to lay out the sketches I had made over the last few weeks and pick the ones to add to my fledgling collection. Pages were moved to one side of the table or the other, depending on whether I thought they were too fanciful or staid or if they were ones most likely to appeal to my ideal customer.

The bell above the door tinkled, and I jumped. The shop had been quieter than a cemetery all week.

Lynn Young stood on the threshold, still clutching the brass handle and with a nervous smile on her lips. "I'm sorry, I know it's getting late, but I happened to be passing and saw the light on. I decided to take the chance that now might be a convenient time?"

"Of course, Miss Young. Welcome to my little atelier." I moved one sketch from the too-fanciful pile and placed it in the middle of the array. It would make a gorgeous feature piece for a bold young woman.

"I doubt I could ever afford anything in here, though." She let go of the handle and the door gently nudged itself shut.

Despite it being summer, twilight came early to Plimmer Steps as the tall buildings on either side stopped the fading sun from reaching the cobbles below. It made it seem much later than the five o'clock the clock signalled on the wall.

Agatha couldn't afford anything either I wanted to say, but I kept that retort buttoned inside me. "I am working on a ready-to-wear line, and I would love to hear your opinion of the direction I am taking with it."

"Wanting the opinion of the common woman?" She injected a lightness into what sounded like an insult about herself.

"The *discerning* woman. A woman who knows quality and fashion but seeks it without the haute couture price tag." A lump formed in my throat. I had promised Sam I wouldn't be alone with her, but I couldn't turn her away when this was my opportunity to learn if she really did do Agatha in. I would simply watch my back and fortunately, I didn't have any shovels. Although there was a pair of lethal tailors' scissors on the cutting table.

I slid the scissors under a drawing, then moved to stand behind her and ran my hands under the collar of the linen coat she wore, to help my newest customer shrug out of the light layer. "I have a couple of dresses you can try on, and as you can see, I am going through my drawings trying to decide what to make."

A shy smile touched her lips, and she peered at the sketches covering the table. Some were fully coloured when my brain said that only a particular colour combination would work with the style. A few had different hues in blocks beside them, to inspire fabric choice. Others were still shaded in grey.

In my mind, I reviewed the dresses and gowns completed and analysed the few encounters we had for clues as to her preferred colours and styles. Then after consideration, I selected two day dresses and one evening gown to show Miss Young.

Long ago, I learned to treat all customers with kindness and courtesy, even if they only bought the cheapest item. Many of us knew the sinking feeling of too few pennies and too many bills. Apart from it being common decency, you never knew when someone might have a change in fortune and remember your kindness or genuine smile. Besides, I found as much pleasure in outfitting a society woman in the latest fashion as there was in finding the perfect dress for a woman on a limited budget.

"Excuse me for a moment, and I'll find the dresses for you to look at." In the storeroom, I pulled down two folded dresses. A cloth draped form in the corner wore an evening gown. I pushed it towards the door, ready to grab when needed. I shook out the first dress. An outfit with a dreamy chiffon outer in pale aqua and white stripes over a solid aqua shift. A strip of white tied the outer closed at the hip and the hemline hit mid-calf.

"Oh, that is pretty." She reached out and plucked at the front. The chiffon was stitched to the soft linen shift, so it only looked like a separate sheer layer over the top. There was no danger of the tie coming undone and the chiffon falling away, leaving a woman almost nude in only the shift.

"Another dress is this one for afternoon calls." I unfolded my version of the pre-war idea of an afternoon gown. Or a pretty dress to wear to receive callers or to make one's afternoon visits. It wasn't a Kiwi practice, yet I infused a slightly more formal line in this dress and thought of it more like Sunday best.

With a square neckline, this dress was a delicately patterned silk in tones of deepest orange and bronze that reminded me of fallen autumn leaves. The long sleeve had a tight cuff with rows of tiny seed pearl buttons. A slightly dropped waist was followed by three layers that created tiers. The last having an asymmetrical hem that brushed a couple of inches above the ankle.

"This is gorgeous, Mrs Devine! I must try this one on, if I may." Lynn's eyes sparkled with excitement.

I had found the right bait for my hook. Now I needed to play a little line as I sought to reel in the information I needed about what happened with Agatha that fatal night. "Of course. If you'll go to the fitting room, I'll bring the dresses."

I gestured to the open door and the room beyond with its full-length mirror and small platform to stand on. As she walked into it, movement outside caught my eye. Sam approached my door. Caught between a potential murderer and my friend, I scrambled with what to do. I couldn't lose this opportunity. I waved my arm at Sam to stop. If the bell chimed, the spell of confidence I was casting between me and Miss Young might break.

Sam paused, confusion written on her face. Grabbing inspiration from the waiting dress form, I mimed raising something over my head and striking it. Repeatedly.

"Is everything all right, Mrs Devine?" Lynn called from the fitting room.

"My apologies, Miss Young," I said in a voice I hoped was loud enough to carry to Sam outside. "The wheel on the dress form is stuck." I grabbed the cloth draped form and pushed it in front of me.

Sam's eyes widened. Then she gave me a thumb's up signal and trotted off. I don't know what she planned to do, but I hoped it involved giving me a bit of time and fetching Joseph.

I closed the door and the outside world disappeared. Layer by layer, Miss Young stripped so I could place the autumnal dress over her head.

Standing on the platform, she turned back and forth, swishing the skirt with her hands. "Johnny would be furious if he knew I was here."

"Oh? Does he not approve of custom-made clothing?" The dress was almost a perfect fit for her, being of a similar shape to the client who had cancelled her appointment for the final fitting. I had finished it anyway, intending to add it to my stock.

"Oh, he has no issue with that. Actually, he's quite the snob and sends his measurements to England. Says only a Saville Row tailor knows how to make a proper suit. No, his problem is with you. All the Marshall family say you did it. What with you being the last one to see her." She turned wide eyes to me and her voice trailed off on the last few words. "Gosh, I hope I'm safe here alone with you."

Funny, I wondered the same thing about being alone with her. By sheer willpower, I held in my explosive retort. Instead, I plastered a smile I most definitely didn't feel on my lips. "I can assure you I had nothing to do with Miss Marshall's demise, and I am sure the detective will find the culprit soon."

"But those were your scissors, weren't they? The ones with the blue and orange thread attached to an S. Found right by Agatha's body. As though they had fallen from your pocket." Her eyes were wide, but her words oddly confident for such a mouse.

I opened my mouth to answer, then slammed it shut. The photograph was black and white. How did she know the colour of the plaited thread hanging from the handle? Nor was it obvious the S related to me, unless someone knew my maiden name. In that instant, I knew it had been her. The day she collected Agatha's dress for her parents. When I fetched the parcel from the storeroom, she must have taken the scissors from my workbasket.

Then placed them in the grass...to implicate me.

The only question in my brain was, did she do it to protect Johnny, or herself?

"Since I was never at Antrim House that night, if they are indeed mine, then Agatha must have taken them on her way out." Needing something to do with my hands, I held up the other dress for her to consider in the mirror.

"I've tried to tell Johnny that I am sure you are innocent. But he does get set in his ways." She turned and a smug smile flashed across her reflection.

Indignation clawed up my throat. I had to strike back but in a polite way, not a physical one. "Has your engagement been announced yet? I can't help but notice the lack of an engagement ring." When she stilled, I undid the buttons to help her shed the dress.

"He is having something fabulous made for me in Auckland. That is why he travels there so often. He says he wants it to be perfect." Standing in her chemise, she ran a hand over the silk of the evening gown.

It appeared she didn't know of his unfaithfulness and intention to marry another. I folded the afternoon dress and placed it on the shelf. "I had wondered if you might have decided to go to America, even after Miss Marshall's death."

Her shoulders heaved. "What do you mean?"

"I had heard that you and Miss Marshall intended to go to America together. It would be a shame to waste your ticket." The rumours spread among my clients could only have come from her, so what was the harm in creating a rumour of my own?

Her hands curled into fists and fire flashed in her eyes. "No! I am not going to America! I will marry Johnny and be the centre of attention for once." Her voice bounced from the walls in the small space. She spun and stepped off the platform, transformed from the malleable secretary into an angry beast.

Our arms brushed against each other as I held out the dress she wore into the shop. The memory from the church flared across my skin again. But this time, as she moaned *no, no, no, not again*...her gaze drifted down to the handle of a shovel clutched in her hands.

Chapter Nineteen

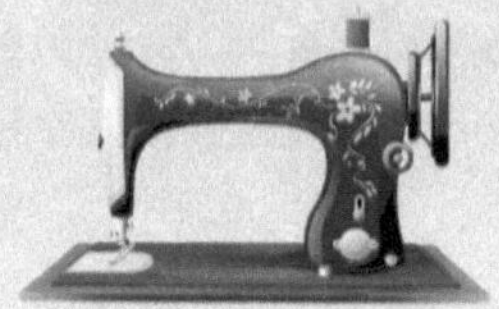

THE AIR WHOOSHED FROM MY LUNGS, AND I FROZE to the spot. She did it. In the heat of an argument most likely. But over what—accompanying Agatha to America? To clear myself of the crime, I needed a confession or something to show the detective. "I'm sorry, I must have misheard. I was sure Agatha mentioned how she was looking forwards to the both of you going to America."

"I hear you are going to expand. Do say I can peek upstairs?" The monster vanished, replaced by a bright light in her eyes and a perky expression.

"There is not much to see. The previous tenants have only recently moved on and we have not turned the space into what I need yet." It was an odd request, and I struggled to re-orientate myself with the conversation. Meanwhile, I hoped Sam wasn't far away with Joseph. This fitting was rapidly getting way out of my depth.

"It's just that I like to design and thought perhaps, to repay your kindness. I could come up with some interior ideas to turn it into something really special." She ran her palms down her skirt as though nervous and she kept glancing at the door.

"If you'd like." I showed her out the shop door, glancing at the end of the lane for Sam and reinforcements as we ducked into the next doorway.

The upstairs had its own entrance, which had attracted me to the idea as it allowed me to separate the haute couture from the ready-to-wear. I pushed on the brass latch and found it unlocked. The tiled entrance also served the other tenants, so most likely one of them left the door unlocked. I kicked a wedge of wood under the door to leave it open, hoping Sam would look for us here.

"This way." I rested one hand on the polished rail as we took the stairs, aware of her steps behind me. Showing a woman who had murdered her friend the deserted floor didn't seem such a good idea now.

The top floor had been broken into smaller rooms and used as lodgings. We intended to turn some into fitting rooms. Others would have the walls removed to create a large work area. What attracted me was the floor-to-ceiling windows at one end, where I intended to position my desk. Before I could realise my dream, I had to get to the bottom of why Agatha's was shattered.

"It's such a shame Agatha never got her chance in Hollywood. I hear the pictures can talk now. Imagine seeing her speaking to us on the big screen. I wonder what she would say?" The movie in my head had Agatha dramatically pointing her finger at her friend and sobbing, *she did it!*

Lynn huffed and ran a hand along the wall. "She'd say fetch my coffee, where is my breakfast, and what appointments do I have today?"

"I have read that stars have secretaries to do all that for them." How much easier to take one with you who was already broken in.

Her movements stilled.

"Did she ask you to go to America with her?" *Or threaten blackmail if you didn't,* I really wanted to say.

Her shoulders heaved, and she clenched her teeth. "Ask? She took it for granted. She said she would break up me and Johnny. Ruin me here, so I had no choice but to go."

Agatha had a beautiful face and a sunny smile, but a rotten heart. The seeds planted over the previous weeks sprouted into life inside me. The newspaper article about the deceased schoolgirl. Agatha collecting secrets and her inability to organise anything. Mintie's comment about the difference between a dream and a plan. Lynn's memory of her sobbing *no not again* and holding a shovel.

Realisation plummeted through me. In the death of the schoolgirl all those years ago, it wasn't Agatha who made the fatal shove. But Lynn.

"She was going to tell Mr Marshall about Kate Burnell and how you killed her," I murmured while taking a step backwards.

"That horrible girl deserved it! Always having to be the centre of attention and talking over the top of me. How was I to know Agatha was worse?" Her shoulders were hunched and her face flushed red.

I had to tell the detective. I raced towards the stairs. Lynn lunged at me, catching the fabric of my floaty sleeve and yanked. It was enough to pull me off balance, fortunately (or not) my construction was sturdy enough to withstand the stress on the seam and it took me a moment to wrench myself from her grasp.

"You killed Agatha, too." Good grief. Would she add a third to her tally? My feet kept walking backwards. The shadow telling me where the stairwell started.

"Nobody is going to stop me from having my time to shine. Not Kate. Not Agatha. And most definitely not you." Then a grin broke over her face and Lynn shoved me with both hands.

An odd feeling of sudden weightlessness encompassed me. In the instant my body tumbled backwards, I couldn't decide if time froze or sped up. My feet scrambled for purchase, but I had backed myself to the top step and Lynn had pushed me down the steep, wooden stairs. There was no stair runner to soften my fall and only cold, hard tiles at the bottom.

An image of Theo and Dad working away on a project made my eyes burn with tears. I screwed them up, partly to deny what was happening and partly because I didn't want to see the floor slam into me. My descent was suddenly arrested as my body lurched to one side. Warmth enveloped me, along with a sense of safety. Oddly, I felt no pain. Strong arms wrapped around me and settled on my skin.

"No!" I cried out. Not in surprise because I was no longer falling, but because I didn't want the memory that surged into my brain.

But it was like no other memory. It didn't push into my brain with a violent thump but instead flowed over me with the gentleness of water. I sighed at the blessed relief from the chaos of the world. There was no colour or noise. As though I had draped my fitting room in black velvet and curled up on the rug.

An old woman appeared, in serene muted hues against the midnight surrounding. Her face was lined from age and wrinkled from laughter. Her hair was pure silver. On her lips, a green-black tattoo swirled over her chin in a distinctive marking. Maori.

She gestured to me, urging me to come closer, nodding and speaking in a lyrical language I didn't understand. A moment of shame flared in my chest.

"I'm sorry, I don't understand," I whispered.

She made a noise and stared upwards for a moment. Then she made a fist with one hand, on the other she fanned out her fingers and put the two together and hopped around before her. "*Pīwakawaka,*" she said.

I stared at the movement, the shape so familiar with a fat little body and a tail proudly displayed. "Fantail!" I cried out in excitement.

She grinned. "*Ka pai.*" Then she spoke slowly, drawing out each syllable. "*Pīwakawaka.*"

"Pī...wa...ka...wa...ka." I haltingly copied her.

Again, the enormous grin took over her face. Then she waved her hands at me, sending me on my way.

"Mrs Devine? Are you hurt?" A commanding voice brought the real world roaring back into my head.

Detective Archer had a firm hold on me and his body was pressed close to mine on the narrow stairs. Warmth and the rich aroma of coffee and something delicious clung to him. It made me want to inhale, like when I stepped into Sam's bakery.

"I'm fine. Thank you." I brushed his hands away while my mind tried to make sense of what I saw. At first, I dismissed it as a memory of the detective as a youngster learning to speak Maori from the old woman. A grandmother of his, perhaps. But this felt...direct. As though my touching his warm skin acted as a conduit, enabling her to speak to me.

"Why were you saying fantail?" He grabbed the balustrade and helped me to my feet.

Words dried in my throat. "Was I? There is a cheeky one that follows me through the Botanic Gardens. How odd I thought of him in my moment of peril."

"But you said it in Maori." Curiosity simmered in his eyes.

Not wanting to answer him, even if that were a question I could answer, I changed the subject. "How are you here?"

Glancing below, Sam stood in the entranceway, her hands clasped and a worried look in her eyes.

"Miss Kostas fetched me, saying you were in some trouble with Miss Young. Intrigued, I accompanied her here, just as you were flung down the stairs." His lips quirked in a smile.

I didn't need reminding of my moment of involuntary flight. "But you must apprehend Miss Young before she climbs out a window. She killed Agatha and that school girl years ago."

He gestured for us to continue up the stairs. "I believe Constable Sullivan has Miss Young in hand."

A dusty Joseph stood on the landing. Miss Young sat on the floor with her hands behind her back and he appeared to be tying them with a length of rope.

Nothing made sense anymore in my shaken brain. "Joseph? How did you get up here?"

He cast me a guilty look. "I had the afternoon off, and your Dad asked me to sneak down and take some measurements for him. When I heard voices, I hid so you wouldn't know I was here. Then, well...it was lucky I was here to nab her after what she said."

"You are mistaken. Mrs Devine did it because Agatha owed her money. She threatened me and I feared for my life," Lynn spoke in a soft tone with wide eyes. Playing the part of the mouse cornered by the scissor-wielding murdering seamstress.

"She took my scissors and put them in the grass." I needed to reiterate my innocence.

"I know. I had searched around the body myself

and knew someone had placed them there to cast suspicion onto you. I had been closing in on Miss Young, but thank you for accelerating my enquiries." Humour gleamed in his dark eyes and he took charge of Miss Young and ushered her away.

Sam rushed up and hugged me. "Are you sure you're all right?"

Once the trio had exited the front door, I turned to my friend. "How did you end up bringing the detective here?"

"No one was home, and he seemed the best alternative. Luckily he was still at the station. He's rather dishy in a quiet and thoughtful way." Sam kept a grip on my arm as we walked down the stairs. Carefully.

A groan escaped my lips. Agatha's death was solved. The true culprit captured. Dishy or not, I never, ever, had to see the detective again.

Chapter Twenty

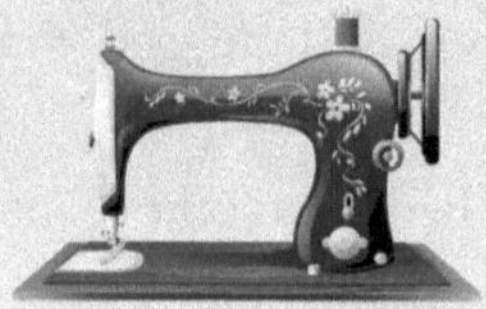

After an exhausting day, I crawled into bed early. That meant I was up early Saturday morning and I sat with Sam in the backyard, watching the birds feasting on the flax flowers.

"I can't believe she killed two people and nearly you as well." Sam had made bacon butties for breakfast and handed one to me.

I wrapped two hands around the sandwich and took a bite of delicious bread, fresh tomato, and crispy bacon. After savouring good food and better friendship, I swallowed. "For once, I am grateful Dad was being sneaky and sent Joseph down to the new premises."

Between us, we pieced together what had happened. Ten years ago, an argument between Lynn and Kate had escalated to the point of a fatal shove. Agatha had witnessed the whole thing and learned that sometimes a secret was worth more than the truth.

Over the years, she used what she saw to mould

Lynn into her secretary. The night of the party at Antrim House, she had dug out the old newspaper article to tell her cousin the truth about that day. Johnny Marshall would have shunned Lynn and possibly she could have been arrested for the long-ago crime. Agatha intended to force the other woman to accompany her to America.

In some ways, I could understand why Lynn snapped. She wanted to live her own life and not spend her allocated years carrying another woman's handbag. "Joseph said Lynn used the fact people overlooked her, to her advantage. She was able to slip out of the party to confront Agatha when she saw her crossing the lawn."

"It's always the quiet ones you have to watch out for." Sam munched on her butty.

We finished our breakfast in silence. Then I licked my fingers, hoping Theo wouldn't catch the waft of bacon on my clothes. My son loved it as much as me. Holding up my hands, I stared at my palms. "Why was I made this way? The memories pushed into my head by those involved didn't help at all."

"Didn't they though?" Sam asked. "Think of what you saw and how they fitted into the overall picture. Agatha's memory hinted at her determination to get to Hollywood. Mintie's memory tried to show you her alibi." Here my so-called friend sniggered at my misunderstanding. "And Lynn's one harked back to the fact she had struck out in anger and killed someone before."

"But none of it was clear. In Lynn's memory, when she muttered *not again*, how was I to know that what she actually meant was *oops I've accidentally killed another one?*" My gift seemed useless to me, and inconvenient.

Sam took my plate and stacked it atop hers. "Perhaps you need to use it more and learn how it works."

I frowned. "How do you use a memory?"

Sam punched my shoulder. "That's what you need to figure out. You've been given a gift in those hands, just like I have in mine. Do you think these hands knew how to knead and shape a loaf of bread when I first started out? Or was your dad born knowing how to turn a piece of wood into a boat? Everything takes time and patience. If you never try to use your gift, of course you don't understand it. Maybe it's time you stopped trying to deny your weird witchy sense and embraced it instead."

I leaned back in my deck chair. Her words made sense. All my life I had tried to deny what Dad said was the trace of magic in my blood. He called my grandmother a witch, but I always thought that simply meant he didn't get on with his mother. Maybe he meant she was literally a witch. What could I do if, instead of being afraid of what I saw, I let the memories wash over me?

"But there are things I don't want to see or know." What if I happened to ask Mrs Cooper to pass me the sugar and she was thinking about her wedding night? A shudder ran through me. Or what if Dad touched me while remembering how he lost his foot or the day mum walked out? I didn't think I was strong enough to take on the pain of others.

"If you look back, I bet everything you've picked up from others has been for a reason. I doubt whatever magic runs through you is there just so you can be a voyeur to imitate memories. What if you are meant to use it to solve crimes, or give comfort to people?" Sam stood and waved to her mother, who appeared at the kitchen window.

"Or perhaps it's so I know exactly what someone wants to look like in a mirror." I took pains not to brush against my clients in the fitting room. But what if any glimpses helped me create the perfect gown for her?

Then the image of the old Maori woman simmered before me. A memory that hadn't been a memory, but something that felt like a real conversation. Why did touching the detective provoke a unique response? I didn't have any answer to that question.

THE FOLLOWING week proved rather busy, once the newspapers ran the article about Lynn Young being apprehended for the murder of her friend. Wednesday, I sat in my chair in the window. A shaft of sunlight managing to angle itself into the lane and strike me for a few brief minutes. A piece of dark red silk sat on my lap as I stitched silver beads into place. Dad made the special tray for beading, with its little wooden compartments to hold each type and colour of bead. The swirling design had taken me days to get right. First, it had to be drawn on paper and approved by the client. Then I transferred it to the fabric in chalk. Once happy with that, I placed a line of stitches to follow. Now came the time-consuming part of gently placing each tiny bead and securing it with even tinier stitches.

Monday morning we had been inundated with people popping in and telephone calls. Once more, my book was stuffed with commissions. King George V's son, the handsome (and single) Edward, Prince of Wales would visit New Zealand in April. Wellington would host both a grand dinner at Government House and a ball. The unmarried socialites of Wellington pounced on their chance at a fairy tale and capturing the prince's eye. The women not only wanted to outdo each other in having the most fabulous frock, but they had also competed for my time.

Those that cancelled were profusely apologetic and wanted to rectify the situation immediately. Some have left it too late to order expensive gowns from Europe and offered significant incentives if I could just fit them in. A few I did, others I had to sadly turn away. The experience with Agatha still stuck in my throat. Never again would I extend credit because of a wide smile and friendly demeanour.

A man walked past and glanced up at the brass lettering above my door. His tailored suit reeked of money even before he pushed inside. Once I glanced at his features, recognition burst into my mind and nerves erupted in my stomach.

"Mr Marshall. How can I help you?" Rising, I placed the silk on the seat of the chair. Worry gnawed at my insides. What trouble was I in now?

He drew an envelope from his jacket pocket and passed it to me. "My family has put you through enough, Mrs Devine, and I'll not have it said we don't settle our debts." He touched his hat and left again.

Sliding a thumb under the flap, I peeked inside to find four, ten-pound notes. My breath whooshed from me.

"Thank you, Agatha," I murmured to the showgirl, wherever she might be.

"Who was that?" Etty called from the back.

"Agatha's father, settling her account." I would take the money directly to the bank. My hands shook at holding so much cash. But I might keep one tenner back. Dad could buy that bike for Theo. Clutching the envelope to my chest, I grinned. Finally, things were looking up and a sense of excitement bubbled through me for what would unfold next.

I HOPE you enjoyed this cosy mystery. You can discover how Grace came to open her business and what secret dwells in her heart by joining the newsletter list, and downloading an exclusive novella at:

https://bookhip.com/KQVTJAW

Grace is drawn into another murder in...
BACKSTITCHED AND STABBED

The only thing worse than wet woollen togs, is a knife in the back...

As the kiwi summer draws to a close, a family outing to the beach takes a deadly turn when a lifeless body washes up on shore. Grace is devastated to recognise the victim, Ricky, who worked in her friend's bakery. But when the supposed drowning victim is rolled over, a shocking truth is revealed—he was murdered.

Drawn into finding the murderer of the cheerful baker, Grace picks at the tangled web of secrets that surrounded Ricky. The man lived a double, or even triple, life. But which version of him had provoked the fatal encounter? Grace and her friends must find the person responsible, before another life is lost to the same tide of violence that claimed Ricky.

To BUY, visit:

HTTPS://TILLYWALLACE.COM/BOOKS/GRACE-DESIGNS-MYSTERIES/BACKSTITCHED-AND-STABBED/

In my early twenties, I moved to Wellington, where I lived on the top floor of an old villa, perched on the edge of the Botanic Gardens in Thorndon. To me, central Wellington always had a cosy feel, due to the way it curves around the harbour and with the hills creating an embrace behind. It's been a delight to set this story where I spent many happy years and peel back its layers of history. I do hope you'll continue this exploration with me in the next book.

Plimmer Steps was named for John Plimmer who came to New Zealand in 1841. He built a house there and the oak tree currently growing on the steps was taken from the original one planted by Plimmer in his garden. I had a building in mind for the location of Grace's business on Plimmer Steps. An odd triangular shape, the Rutland Private Hotel was built in 1917. It once had glorious views of Wellington harbour and the upper floor was indeed used for accommodation. I have changed its ownership and purpose to suit the story. Today there are apartments in the building with large light-giving windows. And it does indeed have a tiled entranceway and wooden staircase to the upper level. There is a brass statue now on Plimmer Steps, of Mr Plimmer and his dog, Fritz, as they stroll from his home down to Lambton Quay.

Kirkcaldies and Stains, or "Kirks" to the locals, is a department store that opened in 1863 and operated until it closed its doors in 2015—when it rebranded as part of the David Jones chain. It always reminded me of a watered-down version of Harrods. Like Grace, I would stare in the window at the luxury goods on display. A uniform-clad footman opened the door for you when you ventured within and shopgirls were on hand to assist with your purchases.

Antrim House is a real place, with its square Italianate tower, completed in 1905 for the Hannah family. Robert Hannah started Hannah shoes (a well-known brand in NZ) and they even manufactured boots for soldiers during WWI. Today the distinctive house is nestled among business buildings, and I must apologise to the Hannah family for setting a murder at their family home. Although I did make sure they were out of town at their farm property that week!

New Zealand never had prohibition, but we had regulations around alcohol, and pubs indeed had to close at six p.m. Restaurants, who served food, were given an extension until eight p.m. The inspiration for the Cricket club comes from a dance hall that operated in Thorndon. The dancers gave lessons by day, giving the club a hint of respectability. Then they performed shows at night—much to the annoyance of their neighbours in the residential area! To skirt the alcohol rules, after 6 p.m. patrons hired a glass, instead of buying drinks.

The Paramount Picture theatre is Wellington's oldest cinema, having opened in August 1917. It was also one of the first theatres to show "talkies" in New Zealand, in the latter half of the 1920s. It's located in the heart of Wellington's entertainment and cultural area.

You may think the idea of a black-market for a breakfast spread is a flight of this author's fancy. (Chapter 6) After the devastating earthquakes in Christchurch in 2011, the Sanitarium factory was substantially damaged and had to close. This resulted in no more Marmite being produced and there was indeed a black-market for the spread in New Zealand. Jars of this stuff went for ridiculous prices in online sales. Personally, I nearly had to resort to eating Vegemite...*shudder*

The Wellington earthquake of 1855 was an 8.2 magnitude that struck not far from the city in Wairarapa. The quake raised the seabed by approximately 1.5 metres (5 feet). This made many of the wharves and jetties on the north-western side of the harbour unusable. There was a silver lining, however, and the new area of land was used for rail. Much of modern Wellington's central business district is built on land raised up by the earthquake. Today, as you walk along Lambton Quay you will find brass plaques embedded in the footpath, showing you where the shoreline used to be.

Over the years Tinakori Road has been home to some of New Zealand's most famous politicians, writers, poets, and artists. At just under 2km (1.1 miles) the history of the road dates back to the mid-1800s. It became a popular area for wealthy, upper-class settlers. What is little known is that the street is not named after someone famous or a wealthy colonist. Its name comes from a dispute between Maori road workers and their employers. The labourers were not given a free meal as part of their pay for working on the road, which was customary. The street subsequently acquired the name Tinakori Road, a mixture of Maori and Pidgin English, which loosely translates to "no dinner road".

The line that Mrs Cooper murmurs in Chapter 12, comes from the poem In Flanders Fields, written by Lieutenant John McCree in 1918.

In Flanders Fields, the poppies blow
Between the crosses, row on row,
That mark our place; and in the sky
The larks, still bravely singing, fly
Scarce heard amid the guns below.

We are the dead. Short days ago
We lived, felt dawn, saw sunset glow,
Loved and were loved, and now we lie,
In Flanders fields.

Take up our quarrel with the foe:
To you from failing hands we throw
The torch; be yours to hold it high.
If ye break faith with us who die
We shall not sleep, though poppies grow
In Flanders fields.

The Shephard's Arms hotel opened in 1870 and was a stop for coaches. Travellers could take refreshments inside, while horses were re-shod at a nearby forge. The pub has withstood the trials of time and to this day, still serves drinks in its original location. It is one of the oldest pubs in Wellington and was my "local" when I lived in Thorndon. Although I must confess I spent more time at the Back Benchers (across the road from parliament), but that's a story for another day!

Also by Tilly Wallace

For the most complete and up to date list of books, please visit https://tillywallacebooks.com

Available series:

Tournament of Shadows

Manner and Monsters

Highland Wolves

Grace Designs Mysteries

About the Author

Tilly drinks entirely too much coffee and is obsessed with hats. When not scouring vintage stores for her next chapeau purchase, she writes whimsical historical fantasy novels, set in a bygone time where magic is real. With a quirky and loveable cast, her books combine vintage magic and gentle humour.

Through loyal friendships, her characters discover that in an uncertain world, the strongest family is the one you create.

Email: tilly@tillywallace.com
Web: https://www.tillywallace.com
STORE: https://www.tillywallacebooks.com

facebook.com/tillywallaceauthor

bookbub.com/authors/tilly-wallace

goodreads.com/tillywallace

www.ingramcontent.com/pod-product-compliance
Lightning Source LLC
Chambersburg PA
CBHW030932210726
48290CB00007B/2158